On the Crow

And Other Stories

BY THE SAME AUTHOR

Washika, A Novel

Robert A. Poirier

On the Crow

And Other Stories

Baraka Books

Montréal

ISBN 978-1-926824-93-2 pbk; 978-1-77186-002-4 epub; 978-1-77186-003-1 pdf; 978-1-77186-004-8 mobi/kindle

Cover by Folio infographie
Book design by Folio infographie

© Baraka Books 2013
Legal Deposit, 4th quarter 2013

Bibliothèque et Archives nationales du Québec
Library and Archives Canada

Published by Baraka Books of Montreal
6977, rue Lacroix
Montréal, Québec H4E 2V4
Telephone: 514 808-8504
info@barakabooks.com
www.barakabooks.com

Printed and bound in Quebec

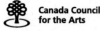

Société
de développement
des entreprises
culturelles
Québec

Baraka Books acknowledges the generous support of its publishing program from the Société de développement des entreprises culturelles du Québec (SODEC) and the Canada Council for the Arts.

Canada Council
for the Arts

We acknowledge the financial support of the Government of Canada, through the National Translation Program for Book Publishing for our translation activities and through the Canada Book Fund (CBF) for our publishing activities.

Trade Distribution & Returns
Canada and the United States
Independent Publishers Group
1-800-888-4741 (IPG1);
orders@ipgbook.com

Contents

To Louise and Pete
(Christmas 2006 to 2011)

After the Portage

Just below the Mànameg rapids on the Mònz River, set back among ferns growing out from porous black boulders, is a wooden cross with a lumberjack's boot sitting on the grave. Grey lichen covers most of the cross and moss grows up from inside the boot. All along the river saturated logs to watch out for lie just below the surface; these are reminders of another time, when men drowned trying to move timber downriver from lumber camps to saw mills hundreds of miles south. What few towns existed then were several days' travel by canoe or horse and wagon, and so the victims were simply buried where they fell. Plain wooden crosses mark their graves. Almost every rapid has at least one.

The Mònz is a gentle river for most of its sixty miles. It is a winding river, twisting and turning on itself, its changing shoreline a constant source of wonder for those who travel upon its waters. There are rapids, of course, and many that must be portaged. It is always a surprise to come upon them, to feel the current carry you forward without effort on your part, to hear the rumblings coming at you from downstream. Sometimes a hasty decision is called for: should you continue on, or pull up on shore and portage around the foaming water, rising and falling, its curling white froth flying upwards and over blackened boulders? And then, almost as suddenly, there is calm water below, looking so much like a wind-protected bay if it were not for the roar behind you.

Anyone paddling the Mònz will soon realize that it is a river of change. From one bend in the river to the next, the feeling experienced is never the same. Along its clay banks are the conifers and alders giving way to cedar swamps further on, with tall ferns growing among the rocks along the water's edge. Here you might find strange-looking carnivorous plants and, between the grey-black boulders, the shockingly beautiful red Cardinal flowers. There are long, sloping beaches of fine sand, from the water line up to plateaus where young trembling aspens whisper in the breeze. Beneath these tall, slender trees, horsetails grow out of the sand like some prehistoric plant life. The sand there is different from that on the beach; the texture is not as fine as beach sand and its colour is a grey-brown, possibly from the aspen leaves decomposing there. Just when you are convinced that you have witnessed all possible combinations, a new shoreline appears just beyond the next bend in the river. The sand shoots upwards abruptly, a vertical wall of compacted sand well over thirty feet in height. There, sparse tufts of grass lean out over the edge. All along its flanks, swallows build their nest holes. Further south along the Mònz, where land was once cleared by early settlers, the river flows lazily among hay fields and lush green pastures where cattle come to browse or lie quietly in the shade of giant butternut trees growing just above the high-water line.

As the canoe came around a bend in the river, the thick alders leaned out over the water and its steep muddy shore and the shoreline changed suddenly to a wall of sand. From the flat water of the river, the bank rose vertically forming a dense wall of compacted grey-yellow soil. As they looked upward from the canoe, the young man and the girl could see the weed heads sticking out over the edge. There were nest holes in the sand along the walls. The swallows poked their heads out of the holes to look at them. The birds grew excited and chattered loudly as the canoe moved in closer.

"I'm tired," the girl said.

"Keep paddling," the man replied. "It'll pass the time."

The girl slammed her paddle against the gunwales. The sound echoed across the water between the two high, sandy banks of the river.

"I don't want to pass the time!" she screamed. "I want to be home, away from this river, and the bugs, and…"

"And me, right?"

"Yes."

Here, the only element of change was the river itself. With every bend in the river came a new sensation, an unexpected emotion for anyone with eyes to see and ears to hear. The canoe advanced slowly between the sandy walls and, without any prior warning, no clue whatsoever, the land dropped down; the Mònz was now a narrow, shallow body of water meandering between gently sloping shores of warm yellow sand with deciduous trees standing tall on flat plateaus above.

The man reached forward with his paddle. He traced a wide arc out away from the canoe and its bow obeyed instantly, moving leftward towards the shore.

"What are you doing?" The girl asked. She looked back as she spoke but she did not look at the man.

The man did not answer. He dipped his paddle into the water and, as he pulled back, he angled the blade outward from the stern; the canoe straightened, flowing parallel to the shore. There was not much water there. There was barely enough water to keep the canoe's wooden keel from dragging on the bottom.

"Jean, what are you doing?"

The man stepped out of the canoe. He rested the blade of his paddle against a gunwale to hold the canoe there.

"Get out," he said.

The girl was on her knees at the bow. She crossed her arms beneath her breasts and stared straight ahead.

"No," she said.

The man tossed the paddle into the canoe. He grabbed the bow with one hand and pulled the canoe up on shore. He reached behind the girl and lifted out a canvas pack.

"Where are you going?"

The man did not answer. She watched him walking up the slope of the beach. His boots slipped in the sand, the long leather laces trailing behind. She could tell that he was angry.

"Jean," she called after him. "Are we going to be here long?"

There was no answer. She could not see him but she could hear him swinging his axe, the sounds of wood being smashed. He was somewhere beyond the row of aspens. There was a clearing there. She had seen it when they came around the bend, after the high walls and the swallow nests.

The girl stepped out of the canoe. The sand was warm on her bare feet. She removed the life jacket and tossed it into the canoe. She hated the thing. She couldn't get a tan with it on and her underarms were red from the jacket chafing her arms when she paddled. But, Jean had insisted. She walked on the sand, close to the water. Pieces of smooth, grey driftwood stuck up out of the sand. The water was shallow there and she could see the bottom, clearly, all the way to the opposite shore. On the upper slope, where Jean worked with his axe, horsetails grew out of the sand and swayed lazily in the breeze. Beyond the horsetails, there was smoke coming from the clearing. She could smell the smoke from where she stood, and hear the wood crackling, and empty pots being jostled. Finally, she decided to go up to the clearing, to see what the man was up to.

As she entered the clearing, she saw the man on his knees with his buttocks resting on his heels. He was adding short lengths of dry spruce to the fire. There were yellow-red flames rising through the matrix of wood he had stacked over a large ball of thin branches and dried grass.

"Here," he said, tossing the small, blackened pail towards the girl. "Get some water for tea."

She caught the pail with both hands. She didn't know why. She dropped the pail to the sand and then looked at her hands; both were covered in soot.

"I don't want any tea," she said.

"There's hot chocolate."

"No."

"And I've got some of that instant orange drink powder."

The girl sighed and looked back towards the river.

"How about a ham-and-cheese sandwich? You could toast it over the fire."

"I'm not hungry."

"Okay, what do you say to a nice, thick piece of lemon meringue pie?"

The girl laughed. She turned, facing the river. She did not want him to see her laughing. Suddenly, she felt his hand on her shoulder.

"Half full," he said, holding the tea pail by its wire handle.

"Oh, all right."

As the girl walked towards the water, she could hear the man whistling and cutting more wood for the fire. She stepped into the water. Her feet sank in the sandy bottom and the water felt cold on her legs. She rinsed the pail twice, holding it against the current by its handle. She submerged the pail, emptied half, and returned to the man and his fire.

There was a large chunk of driftwood by the fire with a green sapling across it. The thick end of the sapling was anchored in the sand while its point reached out over the fire. The man took the pail from the girl and hung it from the point of the sapling.

He reached into the canvas pack. He lifted out a folded, red-chequered blanket and spread it out on the sand away from the fire. Reaching into the pack again, he brought out the plastic bread bags and two cups and placed them on the blanket.

"This here's ham and cheese," he said. He held up one of the bread bags. He pointed to the other bag on the blanket. "That one's boiled egg with little green onions and mayonnaise."

The girl did not speak. She sat on the blanket with her legs crossed and her elbows resting on her knees. She stared at the black-and-red squares on the blanket.

"You can use this," the man said. He held up a long straight branch with a wide fork at one end. "They're good toasted."

She watched him as he placed the sandwich across the forked part of the branch and held it over the fire.

The cover on the pail began to move. He removed the cover. Reaching into his shirt pocket, he took out a tea bag and dropped it into the pail. He turned the sandwich over on the fork. The bread was toasted a dark brown except for two straight lines where the branches of the fork had been. He watched the water churning in the pail: clear, boiling water, then amber, then golden brown. He lifted the pail from the point of the sapling.

"Tea's ready," he said.

He placed the pail on the sand, close to the fire. With a twig he reached into the pail and removed the tea bag, tossing it into the fire. He checked the sandwich; both sides were toasted, and it was hot and burned his fingers, and he juggled it between his hands.

"Here," he said.

The girl held the sandwich between the tips of her fingers and she blew across it and waited for it to cool.

The man filled both cups with tea and set them aside on the sand next to the blanket. He reached into the bag for another sandwich and began toasting it as he had the first.

It was a bright sunny day and what few clouds floated by never seemed to come between them and the sun. It was quiet. There was only the sound of the fire, and a breeze in the aspens above them. The man toasted his sandwich. He could feel the heat of the fire on his thighs and his face as he knelt before it. And he listened to the quiet, as men who live alone do. But he was not alone now. He could feel her presence behind him. Things had not gone well upriver earlier that morning. He smiled as he heard her biting into the sandwich.

The man sat down on the blanket, next to the girl. She had finished eating. She sat with her elbows resting on her knees again, staring at the blanket.

"You want another?"

The girl shrugged her shoulders. She did not look up from the blanket.

The man touched her knee with the back of his hand. The girl looked up at him.

"Here," he said. He held a sandwich in the hand that rested on her knee and the forked branch in the other. "Careful it doesn't fall in."

The girl leaned one hand on his shoulder as she got up from the blanket. She knelt in front of the fire. The heat on her bare thighs was unbearable. She moved back on the sand and held the fork and the sandwich at arm's length over the fire.

After she had finished at the fire, the girl returned to the blanket, sitting cross-legged as she had been before. She slid the sandwich from one hand to the other, blew across it, and finally, she held it with the tips of her fingers and waited for it to cool. The man looked at her. He looked at her, trying to decide if the time was right. The girl glanced up from her sandwich.

"What?" She said.

"Claire, I'm sorry," he said.

The girl looked directly into his eyes and then, as quickly, turned her attention to the blanket.

"I'm sorry I yelled at you," he continued.

The girl said nothing. She bit her lower lip and stared at the blanket. She would cry soon. He knew that. He did not want her to cry.

"Eat up, Claire," he said. "I've got a surprise for you."

It was the only way with Claire. It nearly always worked. If anything can keep her from crying now, he thought, a surprise can. Just the thought of a surprise can do it. He looked at her. Her eyes had begun to tear up but she had started to nibble at the sandwich. The man reached back for the tea and handed her a cup. She took the cup and placed it on her side of the blanket.

"So, what is it?" She said. She looked out towards the river.

"You'll see. Eat."

The man sat with his knees raised and his arms across them and he drank tea from his cup. He looked towards the river where eddies swirled with the current, disappearing almost as quickly. It was really his fault, he thought. There had been absolutely no reason to yell at her like that. After all, it was her first trip. And besides, it was no big deal chasing after the canoe. It wasn't that far off shore and the water was shallow there. He was probably just pissed about going over the portage; him carrying the heavy pack and the canoe on his shoulders while she walked up front whining about the heat and the black flies, carrying a rope and a spare paddle. When they reached the end of the portage and he lowered the canoe into a shallow pool and slipped the pack off his shoulders, he believed that his request had been stated plainly enough.

"Claire, keep an eye on the canoe. I want to take a leak before we leave."

The canoe sat in a quiet pool away from the current but he just wanted to be sure. He walked a short distance from the water and turned his back on the river and the girl.

Just below the rapids, where the man had left the canoe, was a logger's grave. There was a lichen-covered cross and, sitting on the piled stones of the grave, was the log driver's boot with moss growing up from inside it.

"Better take off your boots," the man said, his back still turned away from the river.

The girl did not answer. When he turned to look at her, he saw the canoe floating away from shore. He looked back at the girl. She was leaning over the grave, trying to read the date carved into the wooden cross.

"Claire, for Christ's sake," he screamed.

The girl swung around, rapidly, her lips parted in a sudden intake of air, a look of fear in her eyes.

"What?" It was almost a whisper, barely audible over the roar of the rapids.

"The canoe, damn it," The man screamed again. "What's the matter with you? I told you to keep an eye on it."

The girl stared at the cross. Even the lichen was blurred. Tears swelled over and trickled down her face.

The man zippered up quickly. He removed his boots and jumped into the shallow water. He caught hold of a gunwale and dragged the canoe back to shore.

Now, sitting on the blanket beside her, the pleasure slipped away as he thought about what a fool he had been. He had acted badly. There was no doubt in his mind about that. And there was more to it than almost losing the canoe. His friends had tried to warn him. It wasn't just the difference in their ages; the girl was just too young. They had been together almost eight months. There had been many changes. It was no longer like it had been that first month. Now, they argued, constantly. Claire cried often, even during the night.

"Well?" The girl said.

The man looked at her. She was smiling now, those beautiful hazel eyes with the slightest hint of the Orient. Eyes that formed the bond between them and brought about the first of those silly names only new lovers can appreciate. *"Ma belle,"* he would whisper in her ear. "My beauty with the Malamute eyes."

"Well what?" he said.

"Jean! You promised. You've got a surprise for me. You said so."

"Yes, yes. I know," he said. "Close your eyes."

"Jean!"

"Come on. Close your eyes and don't open them until I tell you."

"Oh, all right."

The girl shifted on the blanket. She sat facing the man, with her eyes closed and her head turned sideways trying to capture any audible clues.

The man looked at her. She was so beautiful. She was beautiful and tanned and he fought the urge to touch her, to brush the silky blond hair from her face, and to kiss her and hold her to him.

"Jean?"

The girl kept her eyes closed. She moved her head to the left and to the right.

"Jean, what are you doing?"

"I was looking at you," he answered.

The girl opened her eyes. The hazel eyes stared into his. There was only the sound of the fire dying, and the river flowing, and now a breeze brushing past her hair.

"Close your eyes, Claire," he said. He looked away from the girl.

"All right," she said. "They're closed."

The man got up from the blanket. He reached into the canvas pack and returned to the blanket. He sat down, facing the girl.

"You can open your eyes now."

The girl opened her eyes. She looked at the man, at the short length of blanket between them. There, on the blanket, was a rose-covered metal canister.

"Open it," the man said.

The girl picked up the canister and pried the lid off. She began to laugh.

"You're crazy!" She said, laughing hysterically.

The man stood up and reached into the pack. He brought out two plastic plates, and two forks wrapped in paper towels and held in place with rubber bands. He set the plates and forks on the blanket. He refilled both cups with tea and sat down, next to the girl.

"Well," he said. "Let's eat."

He reached into the canister with a fork and lifted out a wedge of thick, lemon meringue pie. He slid the section of pie onto a plate and handed the plate and fork to the girl. With a fork he transferred some of the pie to his plate.

"How come, Jean?" The girl said. She was still laughing.

"What?"

"Lemon meringue pie? Come on!"

"It's your favourite."

"And yours too," she said.

"Yes, I suppose."

The girl smiled. She was so very beautiful when she smiled like that. His friends could be wrong about her, he thought. True, she was young, fourteen years younger than he was. But she was mature for her nineteen years. And besides, they had fallen in love and what did years have to do with that?

"So, what happened?" The girl continued. "You're always going on about dehydrated foods, got to keep the weight down, cut out the extras, and all that. Every time you leave on one of your trips, it's always the same."

"It's your first trip," he said. "I wanted you to like it. I wanted so much for you to like it, to want to come with me again."

The girl stared at the squares on the blanket. She began to bite her lower lip.

"Hey," the man said. He placed a hand on her shoulder. He slid his hand beneath her hair and stroked the back of her neck. "What's wrong, Claire?"

"Nothing."

The girl stood up and walked away, down towards the water. She was slipping away from him. He could feel it but he did not want to think about it; that would only make it all the more real. At that moment, there was only the girl and him, and the river flowing. He looked at her leaving, the way she walked on the sand, her back straight and her slim tanned legs and the soft, blond hair falling off her shoulders and down to the small of her back.

"Claire," he called after her. "Come and sit down."

"No."

She did not look at him. She continued walking towards the water without once turning to look at him. The man felt sick inside. It was happening, just like they said it would. His friends had been right after all. He could feel it coming and he did not want it to happen and he knew that he had to do something. She was there in front of him, maybe never again. He got up from the blanket and walked over to where the girl stood, looking at the river. He moved up behind her, close enough to touch her. He placed his hands on her hips and, slowly, he slid his arms around her waist.

"Claire," he said. "I love you."

He could feel her body stiffen as he held her against him.

"Claire," he began again. "Do you still feel the same way about me?"

"No."

The man's arms dropped to his sides. He could feel her hair against his chest and then her warmth left him suddenly as she stepped away. She walked across the sand to the river.

The man returned to the fire and the blanket and the blue plastic plates with thick, lemon meringue pie still on them, uneaten. He poured the rest of the tea onto the fire. He went to the river several times for water, which he poured on the charred remains of the campfire, and on two pieces of driftwood that had been close to the fire. Each time he went down to the river, he looked at her. He hoped that she would look his way, but she stared out towards the river and never turned to look at him.

When he finished with the fire and the smoking lengths of driftwood, he stuffed the blanket into the pack without folding it and, on top of the blanket he tossed in cups and plates and forks, and the wet tea pail. He slipped the sheath over the axe blade and shoved the axe inside the pack. He searched for the rose-covered canister and then remembered that he had left it on the blanket when he bunched it up to throw it into the pack. He picked up the pack and hung it from his shoulder by one of the straps. Coming out of the clearing he saw that the canoe was already in the water with only its stern touching the shore. The girl was on her knees at the bow. She had put on her life jacket and she held her paddle resting across both gunwales.

The man tossed the pack into the canoe. He stepped off the beach, pushing the canoe into the current; holding onto a gunwale, he guided it into deeper water. The water was up to his knees before he finally pulled himself aboard.

The girl paddled steadily. She did not complain of the heat or the bugs. She looked at the shoreline and into the trees. Now, it was all so beautiful. She began to think about what it would be like to paddle down the Mònz again some day. She grew excited just thinking about it, and how her new lover would be, and how it would be warm and pleasant on the beach with someone you love.

The man paddled without any particular rhythm. The river curved upon itself and the swallows stuck their heads out of their nests to look at them but he did not see them. He did not see any of it any more.

Oshkinawe
Sled Dog Race

Saturday was the big day. People huddled together in a single line along the riverbank. Some stood on the ice, on both sides of the starting gate. A prospector tent stood next to the starting gate where hot food and drinks could be had. The people standing around the starting gate sipped hot coffee from paper cups and stamped their feet on the ice trying to keep warm. Although the sun was shining and the sky was a clear blue, a north wind was blowing and the large thermometer next to the tent showed twenty-five below zero on the Fahrenheit scale.

The mayor of the town chatted with the three judges; only his pink frozen face showed through the thick fur of his parka hood. Someone in the tent was trying to announce the names of the contestants over the public address system but the squealing feedback was drowning out his words.

Away from the crowd and the prospector tent, Doctor Callaghan spoke to the eight contestants.

"Now boys," the doctor began, "you know the rules. Once you've started out, there's no turning back, right?"

The flaps of his beaver-skin hat were fastened over his ears. Only his face showed, with his wire-framed spectacles and his round, red cheeks.

"And so even if it takes you a week," the doctor smiled at the boys, "we'll be here. We'll be waiting for you."

The doctor was joking, of course. It was a two-day race and if a contestant did not show at the end of the second day, a rescue party would be sent out to look for him. The boys chuckled nervously. They stamped their feet and twisted their bodies trying to see beyond their parka hoods.

"Doctor Callaghan, sir," a high-pitched voice emanated from the group. "The radio at home says that it's supposed to get colder."

"Is that so? Well, I'll tell you something: while you boys are out there running your dogs just think of the people here freezing their butts off in the cold."

"Yes sir, Doctor Callaghan. But tonight they'll be warm in their homes."

"Yeah," another boy added in support. "We won't be so warm then."

"Now, now, what's all this, eh?" The doctor looked at each of the boys in turn. "You boys are supposed to be bush men, right? Ever hear of a bush man being cold out on the trail. No sir! Each one of you will be bundled up in your tent, with wood crackling in your little tin stove, warm as toast."

When Doctor Callaghan finished speaking, he wrapped the arms of his thick fur coat around each of the boys and wished them good luck on the trail.

Along the steep slope of the riverbank, alders jutted out over the ice. The boys had tied their sleds to the alders and the slender trees jerked violently as the dogs grew excited and lunged forward, barking continuously. Returning to where their teams were tied, the boys yelled at the dogs to lie down. They examined the traces and the round, stuffed collars. It was not uncommon for a restless dog to chew through one of the thick leather traces or, somehow, slip its head out of the collar. The sleds were turned onto their sides so that the steel runners could be checked for slush that might have frozen to them. Each sled had been loaded earlier. The load was covered with a tarpaulin, held down tightly with strips of inner tube. Beneath the tarp was all the equipment required as per the rules of the race: a small prospector tent, a tin stove, a sleeping bag, food for two days, a tea pail, matches, and an axe. Tied to the backrest of each sled was a small canvas bag containing bandages, brown sugar, tea bags, a roll of dried rawhide, and a pocketknife. Each sled also carried a pair of snowshoes.

The first Oshkinawe Sled Dog Race had taken place some thirty years earlier. Doctor Callaghan believed that the race would encourage the formation of character and the physical conditioning of the young lads of the town. He had even convinced the local school board to include the program as an optional course in its secondary level curriculum. Doctor Callaghan's good friend, Cecil Buckshot, visited the school every Friday afternoon, teaching the boys what he knew about living and surviving in the bush. During the last weekend of each month, from September to November, the boys were tested on overnight trips in the forest behind the school. Every second Saturday morning, from December to February, Mervin Lawless would arrive at the school with his team of twelve Siberian Huskies. There, he would teach the boys about sled dogs, how to handle the sled and how to work the dogs out on the trail. Above all, he taught them about respect, the mutual respect that must exist between dogs and their handlers. Without this respect, he told them, nothing good could be expected of the team.

Each young man who showed an interest in the program was invited to visit Mervin's private kennel. During these weekend visits, the boys performed various tasks: feeding and watering the dogs, cleaning kennels, raking the dog yard, hauling in bales of straw for the dog huts, and caring for the pups. Each boy who had proven to be both a serious and capable student was given five Siberian Husky yearlings to raise and train as he had been taught during the program. There was one important condition: if it were discovered that these dogs were being mistreated in any way, they would be immediately returned to Mervin's kennel. Mervin's decision in such cases would be final and nonnegotiable.

Doctor Callaghan and his good friends Cecil and Mervin were proud of the program they had created. They were especially proud of the boys and the effect the training was having on them. Then, one evening at the municipal council meeting, the inevitable happened. The mayor and council decided it was time they had a say in the program. After all, these young boys would be of voting age soon. It was decided that the race should have a proper name. Considering that there was an Indian reserve just south of town and that no one in town was prejudiced in any way, the council agreed to the mayor's suggestion that the race be called The Oshkinawe Sled Dog Race. Oshkinawe is an Algonquin word meaning young man, and so the race became known as the young man's sled dog race. Still, it was a well-known fact that not one of the high school students who lived on the reserve had been encouraged to participate in the program. This was a source of both shame and disappointment for Doctor Callaghan and his two colleagues. They had worked hard to develop the program. It was an integral part of the school curriculum and was totally supported by the people of the town. But there was an overwhelming feeling that they had lost control somehow. Of the three men only Mervin Lawless still had a say in who would handle his dogs, and for how long. Even the name of the race had become an embarrassment, the Oshkinawe Sled Dog Race, with not a single Anishinàbe boy among its participants.

One cold, Sunday morning, the doctor made his way between the high snow banks that lined the path to the Indian church. There were not many people leaving the church. It was very cold and Father Ouellet had run through the mass quickly. Everyone except Father Ouellet had kept their gloves and mitts on throughout most of the service.

As the doctor left the path and walked out onto the road, Cecil Buckshot ran up behind him.

"Hey Doc," he said.

"Cecil," the doctor nodded.

"Everything ready for the Oshkinawe, doc? I got a team, a real fine team. Think I could try out for the race, Doc?"

"Cut out the crap, Cecil," the doctor said without turning to look at him. "You want to come over for a drink or two, fine. But cut out the crap."

"All right, Doc. Still, it's a fine name don't you think? Yes sir, a real fine name."

"All right, all right. That wasn't my idea and you know it," the doctor said. He turned and looked directly into the man's eyes. "But it's a good race, Cecil. Damn it, you should know that better than anyone."

Cecil was the doctor's friend. They had been friends for a long time, even before the so-called Oshkinawe race existed. Doctor Richard Callaghan owed his health and happiness and perhaps even his life to the man.

Back some thirty-four years or so, the young doctor and his lovely wife, Marie, drove into town for the very first time. Their arrival was a most happy event for the residents of the town. The doctor's presence would affect, at some time or other, every man, woman, and child in the community. Doctor Callaghan was the only physician available for more than a hundred miles around. Three years after their arrival, Marie died of tuberculosis. The doctor and his wife had been very happy together and the sudden loss had shattered the man.

One evening, as the sun descended behind the mountain towering over the town, the young doctor stood on the bank of the river, surrounded by alders, and he stared down into the dark water. At his feet was a leather briefcase and, inside it, his bankbook, a land deed, his medical diploma, and a sealed brown envelope addressed to the local notary.

He looked towards the tree tops silhouetted on the mountain and the sun sliding down behind it. He decided that, when the last of the sun had disappeared, it would be time. He thought of Marie, the great and only love of his life. He wondered if they would be together, after.

"Kwe!" a voice called from somewhere on the water.

The doctor grabbed onto an alder. He hadn't heard the man approaching. He had purposely walked several miles from town so as not to be disturbed. The last thing he expected was to meet someone on the river. The man had frightened him. He had come close to falling into the river; such was the irony of his life.

"Hello," the doctor said. He knew that the man was from the reserve but he didn't know his name.

The man made rapid swirling motions with his paddle and the canoe moved in closer, broadside to the shore.

"Hello, Doc," the man said. He held onto an alder branch to keep his canoe from being carried downstream.

It was quiet along the river. Only the frogs sang in the little swamp behind them. The river rippled across a branch that had fallen into the water causing the branch to rise and fall with the passing current. If one listened closely, the magic sound of eddies arose and then, just as quickly, waned.

"How are you, Doc?" the man said.

The doctor didn't answer. He stared at the water and prayed that the man would go away.

"I ran into Jerome Cayer up river. He told me about your wife, Doc. Very sorry for your loss, Doc."

The doctor nodded. He looked at the water and at the man kneeling in his canoe. Then he turned his back on the river and the man in the canoe and he began to cry. He cried openly and without the restraint he had demonstrated at Marie's funeral service or at the cemetery afterwards. Now, the man sobbed with his head and arms hanging down limp.

"I'm sorry," he said, finally, without turning to look at the man. It was dark now and the doctor could feel the coolness of the evening seeping through his suit jacket. He had worn his best suit for the occasion, the same suit he had worn for Marie's funeral. He turned to look at the black, cold water.

"Anibìshwàbo?" the man said, softly, whispered like an eddy as it swirls, flowing downstream with the current.

The doctor was surprised to see the flames of the little fire. The other man had worked silently throughout his crying time. He had not heard him build his fire. The doctor stared at the flames, and at the sparks rising up into the darkness beyond. He had not yet learned the language of the Anishinàbek but he understood the young man's invitation. He moved closer to the fire and sat down beside the man.

"I'm Cecil Buckshot," the man said.

The doctor nodded and extended his hand. They sat together by the fire, like two good friends, drinking tea and listening to the wood burn and feeling its heat on their faces.

During the summer months when Cecil was not on his trap line, he and the doctor spent a great deal of time together. The doctor showed Cecil how to clean and sterilize the syringes and dissecting instruments, and how to drink brandy from a snifter. Cecil taught the doctor how to make fire, and bannock, and how to paddle a canoe. On Sunday afternoons, if it wasn't raining, the two men could be seen paddling up river with their backs straight and not making a sound in the water. From a distance, it was difficult to tell which one of the men was Cecil. There was a joke about town: Cecil was studying to become a doctor, and the doctor might soon be an Indian.

Doctor Callaghan's canoe had become the talk of the town. It was a birch-bark canoe, fifteen feet long. Cecil's father had built it and he had given it to him before he died. Cecil gave it to the doctor one rainy Sunday afternoon.

"It's your canoe now," Cecil said.

"But your father gave you that canoe, Cecil," the doctor protested.

"That's right, Doc. Now, I'm giving it to you."

"I don't know what to say."

"There's nothing to say, Doc. I know that you love that old canoe. But you must have respect for it as well. I know how you have a great respect for those little fires we build along the river, and the peace they bring you. Have the same feelings for this old bark canoe and its teachings will come to you. You see, Doc, you won't really own it. Nobody does. It's just that you've been chosen to take care of it."

The doctor was so very proud of the birch-bark canoe. Any patient who showed the slightest interest was promptly led out to the back shed where the canoe was kept out of the sun and rain. There, the doctor would lift the canoe onto his shoulders to show how light it was. He would explain to his patient how its covering was a winter bark, how the lacing consisted of split spruce roots, and how his friend, Cecil Buckshot, was the best canoe man he had ever known.

One windy Saturday afternoon, during that dry period between spring and summer, two young boys set fire to the tall, dead grass in the field behind the doctor's home. The wind carried the flames across the field towards the doctor's house. From inside his examining room, Doctor Callaghan could hear the sounds of men's voices. When he looked out the window, he saw the smoke, and flames, and men coming from all directions. The men carried shovels, and some of the men held large spruce branches that they used for beating down the flames.

The townsfolk spoke of that day for a long time afterwards. They liked telling about how Doctor Callaghan had come rushing out of the house, chasing his patients out onto the sidewalk and then, how he ran back towards the fire and disappeared in the smoke. There was no sign of the man after that. It wasn't until the fire was brought under control and the smoke had cleared away that they saw him. The doctor was standing by the road, away from the burned-over area, with a birch bark canoe resting on his shoulders.

Doctor Callaghan was the most respected man in town. He was impeccable both in manner and dress, attended Sunday services on a regular basis and, although stern, he was a most gentle and caring physician. He was, however, known to be eccentric at times. There was often a great deal of humour involved in the doctor's activities. One particular event occurred thirty some years before the Oshkinawe race. During the last week of December of that year, Doctor Callaghan instructed his house keeper, Mrs. Irene Henderson, to cook a large turkey with stuffing, several meat pies, cookies of all sorts, and a large tin of plum pudding. These he packed in a sturdy wooden box along with sauce for the pudding, several bottles of pickles, the bread-and-butter kind that Mrs. Henderson made herself, and cranberry sauce for the turkey. Wrapped in thick wool socks, he included four bottles of his best brandy. He hired Mervin Lawless with his team of Siberian Huskies and on the twenty-third of December they set out by dog team to join Cecil on his trap line for the Christmas holidays. The plan was simple enough. Mervin was to take the doctor up to Cecil's cabin, spend the night there, and return to town the next day, in time for Christmas with his family. He would return to Cecil's cabin on the second of January, to bring the doctor back to town.

The first night at Cecil's cabin, they ate and drank and got so tight that Mervin was not able to get around the next day. After a quick check on the food that was left, and the number of beaver carcasses available for the dogs, Mervin decided to stay on with Cecil and the doctor until it was time to return to town. Actually, Mervin had spoken to his parents before leaving, that there was a strong possibility that he might spend Christmas with his two friends in the bush.

The doctor and his friends had a wonderful time together. After they sobered up, they went out on Cecil's line to check the traps. The doctor made fire on the trail, and he prepared bannock and tea. He handled the team while Cecil and Mervin worked off the trail on snowshoes. In the evenings, they sat by the cast iron stove, listening to Mervin's stories and enjoying Doctor Callaghan's choice brandy.

One cold, clear night, they slept out on the trail. The doctor tightened the blankets around him, turning the colder part of his body towards the fire. He listened to the wood as it burned and smelled the balsam branches beneath him. As he lay there by the fire an idea came to him, a sudden awareness, as certain as the darkness that creeps upon you at the end of a winter's day. It possessed him completely and would not leave him. He stared up at the snow-laden conifers and the stars above them. It was all there, clear and precise, every minute detail; how the race would be, how old the boys would have to be, the training they would receive, and the equipment they would need. Everything was there. The idea itself would not allow him to sleep, and he didn't want to sleep just thinking about it.

It had been a long time since he had been so excited. He would do it. He decided that night that he would do it for the young boys of the town, and for Marie. In the morning, as soon as he heard them stirring in their blankets, he would tell them about it; how each of them would contribute to the plan, how wonderful it would all be. The doctor stared at the dying embers of the fire. From somewhere behind him he heard a tree trunk cracking from the cold. Inside his warm blankets, Richard Callaghan smiled in the dark.

Thirty years had gone by since that night on the trail, thirty long wonderful years. The doctor was an old man now. And Cecil was gone. He died, asleep in his blankets, one night when the temperature dropped to seventy-five below. But, he had died in the bush. There was that, at least, and the doctor was happy for him.

Today, the doctor stood at the starting gate with the mayor, the very same mayor who had come up with the name, Oshkinawe Sled Dog Race. Mervin Lawless was one of the judges, as he had been since the beginning of the races. He no longer had any dogs of his own. When anyone asked him what he thought of the dogs gathered there for the race he would always answer that the best dogs he had ever known were now six feet underground.

A strong wind continued to blow from the north. This added to the cold and caused the banners above the starting line to point steadily south. The contestants approached the starting line, one at a time, and at five-minute intervals. Each boy stood behind his sled with one foot on the brake, keeping a close watch on his team and waiting for the countdown to end. At the end of the count the judge yelled, "Go!" and, each time, the doctor held his breath; would the dogs lunge forward as expected or would they swing sideways towards the crowd lining the starting gate? Worse still, would the dogs get tangled up in their traces and a fight start, disqualifying the young man and his team?

There were no incidents at the starting line. The teams were off, each in turn, and the doctor watched them going down the trail on the river. He could see the young driver's back and the heads of the dogs bobbing as they loped forward. They would not lope for long. He knew that. A mile down river, the trail went up a steep bank and then up the side of the mountain overlooking the town. The people standing on the bank of the river could still see the teams going up the mountain if they used binoculars. They could see them on the bare patch just as the boys went over the crest of the mountain. After that, the boys and their teams would disappear from view and begin the swift ride down the other side of the mountain and into the cedar swamp.

The doctor knew the trail well. He and Cecil had mapped it out together years ago. They had walked the trail on snowshoes and, when it got too long to be walked completely in one day, they'd head out with Mervin and his team. They worked with buck-saw and axe, cutting and pruning, and cleaning up branches afterwards. Now, it was a clean, wide trail through cedar swamps and over mountains of hardwood and pine, and spruce and balsam in the lowlands.

To the boys and their teams, it was fifty miles of snow and cold. There were long climbs up bare hardwood mountains where they had to run behind the sleds, and frozen swamps in the lowlands with cedar and the dangerous wet places. There the slush sometimes froze to the runners, and often the dogs' foot pads would bleed.

As the doctor watched one of the contestants speed down the trail and disappear behind a bend in the river, the announcer's voice cut through the wind.

"Alvin Vincent!" the voice called. "Alvin Vincent at the starting gate, please."

The young man and his team approached the starting gate. His was the last team to head out. Alvin rode the sled, keeping one foot on the brake. Another boy walked ahead of the team, holding on to the lead dog's collar.

The doctor smiled. Alvin was Henry Vincent's boy. Henry was one of the boys who had set fire to the grass behind his house and almost burned his canoe. That was so long ago, he thought to himself, still it seemed that only a short time had gone by. Cecil was gone as was the bark canoe. The doctor had given the canoe to Henry Vincent. That day, when Henry arrived to pick up the canoe, he could not let it go without a few parting words.

"Take good care of it, Henry," he said. "You won't really own this canoe, Henry. Nobody does. You've been chosen to take care of it. Have respect for this old canoe and its teachings will come to you."

The next day, the second day of the race, was as cold as the first. Still, the people were there, lined up along the riverbank or standing on the ice at the starting gate. They were there to see the teams arriving, to applaud and cheer them on. Sometimes there would be groups of two or more teams returning, some teams loping while others were plodding along at a slow trot. The boys handling the sleds stood with one foot on a runner and pedaled with the other, pushing the sled forward each time their foot hit the snow.

At the starting gate, the judges noted the arrival time of each team and the boys' names were announced over the public address system as the people applauded and cheered. Shortly after the last team arrived, a call to attention was heard over the loudspeakers. Alvin Vincent had completed the race with the best time overall. The times for the seven other teams were announced. All teams received equal applause. To the people of the town, all eight contestants were winners and each of the boys would receive a trophy for his efforts. The boy with the best time would receive the Mervin Lawless Trophy, the boy with best looking team earned himself the Cecil Buckshot Trophy, and so on until all eight boys were rewarded for their good work. Each trophy was presented by the person whose name was attached to it: Mervin Lawless presented the Mervin Lawless Trophy, Cecil Buckshot's widow, Angie, presented the Cecil Buckshot Trophy. Even the mayor got to present a trophy as did all of his councillors. There was a ninth trophy, the Richard/Marie Callaghan Trophy that was presented to the contestant who had demonstrated the greatest kindness and care to both his dogs and his fellow contestants, who showed the utmost respect for his elders and teachers, and whose ultimate goal was not the winning of a race but rather being part of it, of contributing to its very existence.

After all eight trophies had been presented and the applause had ceased, the crowd waited with great expectation. Who would be this year's recipient of the Richard/Marie Callaghan Trophy? The eight contestants stood by the starting gate, clutching their trophies and waiting for the announcement. Mervin Lawless walked up to the microphone. He removed his beaver skin hat and looked out at the crowd.

"I've got some bad news," he began. "Doctor Callaghan won't be here to present his trophy. Sometime during the night our good friend passed away in his sleep. I spent a couple of hours with him last night. We shared a few drinks and we talked about Cecil and the Oshkinawe. He was so proud of this race. He told me who he had chosen for the

Richard/Marie Trophy. He was so happy to tell me the boy's name."

Mervin stopped speaking. After a short time he cleared his throat.

"I'd like all of you to think back on the ideas upon which this race was created," he continued. "The training that the boys receive is not only about winning a race. They learn about respect for their elders, for their fellow contestants, for the dogs on their team, and for all of the other teams. The boys who participated in this year's race, and in past races, should be properly recognized for their courage and their hard work. But what about the other boys, those boys who have never been chosen to participate in the program? There are probably many of you out there right now who dream of being a part of this race someday. Doctor Callaghan met one of you during this past year. I also got to know this young lad, a shy and gentle boy whose love and respect for his elders goes mostly unnoticed. He has come here today with his grandparents, at Doctor Callaghan's request."

The crowd stirred. People glanced sideways and around them. Some of the older ones had tears in their eyes.

"I won't hold you any longer," Mervin began once again. "You know, this young boy has a fine team of dogs and he travels the bush trails behind his home every day. He snares rabbits for his grandmother's stews and gathers birch bark and cedar kindling for his grandfather's fires. He's a fine lad who treats his dogs with the same kindness and respect that he has for all his relatives and friends. This year's Richard/ Marie Callaghan Award goes to Mister Richard Buckshot."

Cheering and applause arose from the crowd. A young boy moved forward, walking slowly towards the prospector tent and Mervin Lawless who held a large trophy with both hands. The boy was accompanied by his grandmother, Angie Buckshot, and his maternal grandparents, Tom and Helena Nottaway.

The Enforcer

Sitting on the wet concrete, just below the over-pass, he could hear the speeding cars on the highway but could not see them. He could see the large street lamp above him and the colour it imparted to his skin: what his skin would look like when he was dead. Whenever a car exited the highway and came speeding down the off ramp, he could hear it, and then its slowing down as it approached the stop sign. He would stand up then, and hold out his thumb and see the headlights coming towards him. The stop sign was the critical point. If the driver moved off slowly there was a good chance that he would stop. However, the driver could accelerate and drive past him with a cold stare. That would leave him spitting on the pavement, feeling dejected and cold once again as he sat down on the rough, wet sidewalk.

It had been pleasant enough at the Carrefour that night. Lewie had been good to him. He did not have to repeat that he wanted only one ice in his drink. There was no need to explain that this was one of those nights, a time when he needed to be alone to build up those walls that he needed to see himself as he really was.

"There you go, monsieur Karl," the man said. "One ice, one bourbon, nothing more."

The man turned and walked to the far end of the bar. There was no need to talk. There were other nights when both men would speak, discussing the morose subjects on their minds. This was not one of those nights.

The bar was full. There was not a single space along its length, people stood three deep in places, heads bobbing, some trying to speak above the music coming from the jukebox, beautiful smiling bodies. There were faces he remembered from late April, during the final exams. They were not smiling then. Now, they were so cool, not a worried face among them. He wondered if the student who had called in the bomb threat during an evening exam at the gymnasium was there, shaking and bobbing with the rest of them. He probably moved on to another campus, or maybe he was working at the Market now, cleaning fish maybe. The ice was melting. Karl shot back what was left of his drink and made signs to Lewie for another, with a beer chaser.

The Carrefour was a schizoid bar. In front of the bar was a well-lit room with a jukebox where you could be wild and crazy and start a fight or two. Next to the jukebox was a heavy plank door with wrought-iron strap-hinges. When this door opened, it could only mean one thing: a fight was brewing and Lewie had tapped the little white button taped beneath the bar, a signal for Gaetan that his services were required. Gaetan was a powerful brute of a man. He worked another bar in the hotel complex, one of five bars in total. But his little bar was special in that it had tunnels leading to the four other bars. When things got out of hand, he was called upon to set things straight. It was simply a matter of selecting the right tunnel and making his presence known wherever the trouble was. As Gaetan made his way through the tunnel his blood pressure and his adrenaline level would climb, his heart would begin to pound rapidly beneath his fake dinner jacket. When he slammed open the plank door and stepped into the lighted room, two things were on his mind: how many were there and how far could he go in settling things?

There was a back room in the Carrefour. This was a sombre, smoke-filled room where you could spend an entire evening getting drunk without uttering a single word. There was an upright piano at one end of the room that no one ever played, or hardly ever. Dope was often stashed there. Some nights a guitar and singing could be heard. There were folk songs, and sometimes a dude pounding on the piano and sounding like Bob Dylan. You could always count on a dull murmur coming from each table but low enough so that you did not even try to listen.

Karl had been there the night before. Or was it the night before that? He could not remember. The back room of the Carrefour was like that.

"Hey man, spare some change?" A voice from another table, somewhere next to Karl's.

"No," Karl answered without looking up.

"Cool," the voice replied.

Karl was organized. He was not happy in his life but he was organized. Even his most depressed moments displayed order of sorts, down to the last detail. He sat there, his left leg crossed over his right, both arms crossed at the wrists and resting on his thigh, just above the knee. Everything was perfect. He was at his favourite wooden table, facing the wall, cigarettes and matches by the ashtray, his bourbon and beer chaser an easy right-hand swing away. He sat there somewhat content, at least not unhappy, in his solitude. He began to organize his thoughts. Tonight would be different. Tonight, he would drop his bummed-out feelings of how empty his life was and what a loser he had been for the last six years. Tonight, he had other things to deal with, someone he must speak to. Not just anyone. Otto was the man he needed. Otto would be able to help him out on this one. But where was Otto? Was he still in jail? Or had they let him out again? It was never easy when they let him out. He had to learn to save up the methadone for a decent fix. Besides, things outside had changed. The guys were not the same. They wore their hair long now and, often, he could not make out what they were saying. To Otto, they were all fat cats, fat cats living in a world far removed from his own.

Karl was into his fourth bourbon and beer chaser when Otto arrived. His arrival in the back room, the icy stare and that thin-lipped smile, always had the same effect. He was simply checking out the crowd, who might be dangerous and who were those he could ignore. But the people looked away, not wanting direct eye contact with the man, fearing that they might instill some degree of aggression in the recent parolee; some began rolling cigarettes, others checked the time, anything but direct eye contact. No one ever stared directly into the eyes of the Alpha wolf. No one, that is, except Karl. And that is probably why they got on so well.

Otto nodded as his gaze met Karl's. He walked by the other tables, speaking to some of the people, standing with his glass and quart bottle in one hand. He joined Karl then and sat down across the table from him, with his back to the wall.

"Hey there, Karl," he said. "How's it going my friend?"

Friend? Otto had called him his friend. Karl never responded to the compliment but it always made him feel good inside.

"Not bad, I guess," he said.

"What do you mean, not bad?" Otto stared at him. "What's wrong with you guys? You got it made here. You guys don't know what trouble is."

"Yeah, I suppose. What's with your head?"

From the time he had sat down, Otto kept his left hand cupped over the top of his head. When Karl mentioned it, he took his hand away. The palm of his hand was covered in wet, glistening blood.

"Nothing," Otto replied.

"What do you mean, nothing? Shit man, you're bleeding."

"Take it easy, Karl. It's just a cut."

"Oh yeah? So how'd that happen?"

"Hash. Supposed to meet a guy. Two showed up."

"They get away with the dope?"

"No. And I got the cash."

"They paid, and you still have the hash?"

"Yep."

"So, what's with the blood? You okay?"

"Sure. He handed over the cash and I knifed him in the gut. It was him or me. That's when the other one got me with the bottle. They ran away after that."

Otto filled his glass. He took a handkerchief from his jacket pocket and wiped his hand clean.

"So, what's happening with you?" he said. The discussion was over. Karl knew Otto well enough to realize that any more talk about dope deals and blood would only make him nervous. Nobody wanted Otto to be nervous.

"Not much," Karl answered. He took a long drag on his cigarette and inhaled deeply. The smoke was long in coming out of his mouth. "Ran into some heavies a couple nights ago. You know."

"No, I don't know."

"Wasn't much, really. I was hitching a ride home, after closing time. Got a ride just near the overpass.

Pretty heavy dudes. Two of them. Been in jail and all. Told me how they beat up on a screw. They even mentioned the joint they were in but I forget the name."

"Punks," Otto said, emptying his glass.

"No kidding, man," Karl continued. "These guys were tough. Said they'd been in more than one pen."

"Listen Karl. Listen to me good," Otto leaned across the table. "You guys don't know what tough is. How could you? Believe me, those guys were nothing but punks. Shit-heads trying to scare you."

"Think so, huh? Man, I don't know. The way they described that prison guard they beat up, and how they got away with it."

"Don't believe it," Otto said, filling his glass from the quart bottle. "These creeps have a name?"

"I didn't ask."

Otto leaned back in his chair. There was that infamous thin-lipped smile once again that, in Otto, could be interpreted as slight amusement or just about ready to strike. In any case, both could be considered as symptoms characteristic of Otto's sometimes twisted personality.

"Ever see them again," he said, "just mention my name. Just say you know me; that we're buddies from way back. If they've been inside, they'll know me."

"What if they've never heard of you? What then?"

"Then they're lying. They're just cheap punks having a little fun with you."

Just about everyone in the back room of the Carrefour knew about Otto. He had been in and out of prison since he was a teenager: reform school, city jails, penitentiaries, both minimum and maximum. He spoke to Karl about it one slow night at the Carrefour. It all began with his dad, Otto said, when he was ten or eleven years old. A man has to be able to fight. That was his dad's idea of life. If you couldn't fight, you were a loser and no son of his would grow up to be a loser. So, there were boxing matches in the alleys, without rules of any kind, and the fights only ended when one of the two boys was knocked senseless or his dad decided that they both had had enough. After having his nose broken and both eyes blackened, Otto finally tired of being beaten up all the time and having his dad calling him a god dam sissy in front of the other boys. So, he trained hard at the gym and he did barbells in his room at night. Before long, he was dishing out the punches, breaking noses and closing eyes. His father stopped calling him a sissy but he never once visited Otto at the reform school or any of the other institutions where he was doing time. When he was inside, Otto trained every day, working out on the heavy bag and lifting weights and perfecting his fighting techniques. All of this hard work was soon put to good use. Not a day went by inside when Otto was ever short on heroin. And it never cost him a dime. There were rules inside and it took guys like Otto to make sure they were followed. These were not prison rules.

These were laws put forward and enforced by the incarcerated. Being outside proved to be more difficult. Saving up methadone for a decent fix was never easy. Also, most of the guys he trusted were inside, not on the street. Otto was a street fighter. A shrink inside once claimed that Otto was a psychopath and that's where his fighting style came from.

"Anyway," Karl said, "I think I'm going to start carrying a knife. There're all sorts of crazies out there at night."

Otto fixed his eyes on Karl's. His pupils were not the contracted black points they were when he overdosed on methadone, or when he had managed to find some good heroin. Now, the pupils of his eyes were large and black as he stared steadily into Karl's eyes.

"Be sure you're ready to use it," he said.

"Sort of like pointing a gun, isn't it? I mean, me pulling a knife out should warn a dude to back off."

"Depends. Pull a knife out like that on me, and you're dead. For people like me, some guy waving a knife in my face just says, I'm going to kill you. So you stick him first. Like that asshole tonight."

Karl finished the bourbon. He still had half a quart of beer left. He stood up from the table.

"Another beer?"

"Sure," Otto replied.

Karl left, carrying his empty shot glass. As he approached the bar, the bright lights strained his eyes. The loud voices and the blaring jukebox stirred up an aggression in him that he had not felt all evening. Just standing at the bar, waiting his turn, filled him with feelings of violence, a violence that he was not capable of acting upon but which was there nevertheless.

"Hey man," the words came from behind him. "Having a heavy rap with your friend Otto?"

It was Stéphane, the most sarcastic, morbid person that Karl had ever known. Now, with his usual condescending smile, he added emphasis to the word, "heavy."

Karl signalled to Lewie for another bourbon as he placed the empty glass on the bar.

"And a beer," he added.

He turned to look at Stéphane. He stared into the man's eyes without smiling.

"Stéphane," he said, "you have no fucking idea what heavy is."

Karl turned his back on Stéphane, paid for the drinks, and left.

"What's with him?" Stéphane tried to save face.

Lewie said nothing. He closed his eyes briefly, shaking his head as if to say, "I don't know. I don't want to know. Mind your business. Don't even think about it." Karl had heard those very words from Lewie on numerous occasions, as had Stéphane and most of the crowd from the back room. With them, he had only to close his eyes and shake his head from side to side; the message was clear.

Karl was pleased with his little put down on Stéphane. It was usually the other way around.

Stéphane had an extensive vocabulary and he used words like punches and nearly always won out over the poor sucker he was picking on.

As he sat on the wet concrete by the stop sign, Karl smiled in his solitude. He could hear the bugs buzzing around the mercury lamp. It was that time, between late evening and early morning, when barroom floors have been swept and chairs are stacked on tables, not a sound on the boulevard and traffic lights changing colours with no one to care. Karl sat with his knees up and his elbows resting on them. It had been a good night. Otto left before last call. Some errand that couldn't wait, or he couldn't wait. Karl wasn't sure. Otto did a lot of heroin. That was all he knew.

Karl had slept, sitting there on the sidewalk. He didn't know how long. The mercury lamp was still lit but he could hear traffic on the overpass. He guessed that it must be early morning, closer to dawn. A set of headlights approached the intersection. Karl stood up, holding his thumb out and feeling his damp trousers sticking to his buttocks. The car slowed at the stop sign but kept moving out onto the highway. The car went past him, slowly, and then stopped suddenly. He could see the clear part of the rear lights brighten as the driver shifted into reverse.

"Where to fella?" The words came from an open window on the passenger side.

Karl ran up to the car. He grasped the rear door handle.

"What's the matter? You deaf?" The man screamed at him. "I said, where to?"

"About ten miles," Karl answered. "North."

"Okay then, get in."

It was not until he sat inside the car and recognized the smell and the blue driving lamp in the upper left-hand corner of the windshield that he realized these were the same guys, the same creeps that tried to scare him only a few nights before. They even wore the same clothes. The man on the passenger side was smoking a cigarette and he held a beer bottle in his left hand.

"You working nights?" he said without turning around. "You here every night?"

"No, not every night," Karl replied.

The man turned to look at him.

"Hey Gino," he said to the driver. "Remember him?"

The driver looked back at Karl.

"No. Should I?"

"Come on, Gino. We picked up this twit two nights ago. He's a juicer, can't you tell? Hey fella, got any bills left, huh? You know, cash. Got any money left?"

"No," Karl answered.

"Should hang out with us. Plenty of cash where we go."

"Cut it out, Frank!" The driver stared at the man. He looked at Karl in the rear-view mirror. "So fella, what's your name anyway?"

"Karl. Your name's Gino, right?"

"Yeah. What's it to ya?"

"Nothing. Just heard him call you Gino."

"So," the driver said, "we picked you up before. Remember us?"

"Oh sure."

"Tell me," the driver looked at him in the mirror again. "What we talk about?"

"Well," Karl looked at the driver and then at Frank. "You were talking about a prison guard, a screw I think you said, and how you beat him up real good. Then you mentioned some of the prisons you'd been in."

"Anything else?" The driver turned to look at him.

"No, I don't think so."

The conversation seemed to end there. Karl sat on the back seat, in the middle, so he could see the road. He didn't want to miss the turn to his place. Besides, the driver appeared to be having trouble with the curves in the road.

"You sure you ain't got no cash?" Frank turned to face him. "We could check, you know."

"He wouldn't lie," Gino said. He looked at Karl in the mirror. "I mean, we tell you all about us and everything."

"Yeah," Frank added. "You know all about us, being in the pen and all. You know what we do to stools. You know about that, right?"

"Yeah sure," Karl said. "Of course I know about that."

He could not see their faces clearly. It was dark in the car, even with the dash lights and the blue driving lamp. Karl was trying to decide how serious they were. Or were they just screwing him around like Otto said?

"I've got a friend who knows plenty about that stuff," he said. "I learned lots from him."

"Yeah, I'll bet," the driver said.

"Tough guy, huh?" Frank chuckled. "Mention our names next time you see him."

"Yeah," the driver added. "Franky and Gino. See if he turns pale when you mention our names. Ha! Ha! Ha! Ha! Ha!"

"Hey, that's pretty funny," Karl felt better. He actually felt like laughing. Otto was right. Punks! Just cheap punks.

"Oh yeah, what's so funny, wise guy?" The driver struggled with a curve in the road.

"Well, it's kind of funny, you telling me to mention your names to my friend," Karl explained. "You see, he told me exactly the same thing. He said that if I ever ran into you guys again, I should mention his name. Pretty cool, huh?"

"Yeah, real cool," Gino said. "What's this jerk's name anyway? Anybody we should know?"

"Probably," Karl began. "I mean, seeing that you guys been inside and all. My friend too. He's been inside a lot."

"Right, the driver said. He looked over at Frank. "What do you think, Franky? Think we should kinda pull over and have a little chat?"

"Well, ya know Gino, I'm kinda curious about this friend of his. Maybe he'll tell us when we empty his pockets. What do ya say guy?"

Now was the time. Karl had no doubts about Otto's reputation. If these two hoods were anywhere near as tough as they pretended to be, they would have heard of him. Karl remembered some of Otto's "associates" who dropped into the Carrefour from time to time. They wore suits and ties and, when they reached into their shirt pockets for cigarettes, the tan coloured straps of their shoulder holsters showed. Otto chuckled later as he assured everyone that these guys were not cops.

"His name's Otto," Karl began. "Otto Felding. Actually, we been friends since we were kids. Don't see him much these days as he spends a lot of time inside. But I was with him tonight. I told him about meeting you guys. That's when he said to mention his name if I ever ran into you guys again."

"Okay," the driver snapped. The car slowed down and the driver pulled over onto the shoulder of the road. "Out you go, my friend. This is where we dropped you off last time, right?"

That's right."

Just beyond the car, Karl could see the large lighted area and the motel-restaurant, and the side road that led to his cabin less than a mile away. He opened the door and stepped out of the car.

"Franky," the driver said. "Give him a beer and a couple of smokes."

"Yeah, sure thing."

"You take care now," the driver said. "And you say to Otto that we said hello, ya hear."

"No problem."

Karl slipped the cigarettes into his shirt pocket. The beer was almost ice-cold in his hand as he watched the car speeding away, its rear lights a bright red in the almost light of day.

On the Crow

The river flowed unnoticed for thousands of years. One day, a group of people pulled their canoes up onto its shore. Was it to bathe, or to fish, or perhaps to bury one of their own? Whatever the reason, the people stayed. After they pulled their canoes ashore and set up camp, no one had a desire to leave.

It wasn't long before someone gave the river a name. They called it Àndeg Zibi. Nobody knew why. That was the river's name and, according to the elders, Àndeg Zibi had always been the river's name.

From that time on, the river was a source of food and water, a means of transportation, and its shores a quiet place of meditation for the people of Àndeg Zibi, or the Àndeg Zibi Anishinàbek. It was not a sudden thing. An occasional white trapper was seen paddling upstream. Rifle shots were heard in the distance. Early one morning, they heard the ring of an axe coming through the forest. A dirt road soon appeared along the shores of the Àndeg Zibi, on their side of the river. Groups of young men arrived, walking or driving carts pulled by horses. Soon after came men and women in horse-drawn wagons. The wagons were heavily loaded and the metal-shod wheels left deep tracks in the road. The settlers moved slowly along the dirt road and the Àndeg Zibi Anishinàbek examined them as they would some strange, new animal.

New settlers arrived almost daily. They set up their camps a little more than two miles north of the community. Still, life along the Àndeg Zibi remained relatively unchanged for the Àndeg Zibi Anishinàbek. The young men paddled upriver during the spawning time of the pickerel and some went fishing for bass in the deep-water places along the river. During the fall, hunting parties paddled their long bark canoes north in search of moose for their winter food supply. Winter was trapping time and young men travelled to their trap lines on snowshoes, with packs on their backs or hauling supplies on narrow toboggans northward on the frozen Àndeg Zibi. They spent weeks, sometimes months, in the bush and some stayed there all winter, returning just before breakup in the spring.

But changes do occur, sometimes so slowly that we fail to notice them. Gradually, changes were brought to bear upon the Àndeg Zibi Anishinàbek. That they could no longer leave their canoes without worry of them being stolen was a minor detail. That they had to portage their canoes across the rusty railroad tracks, a recent addition to the settlers' way of life, and then walk through the muddy dirt road before setting their canoes down in the water, was not a major issue either. Nor was the proximity of the new settlement to their community a source of trouble. It wasn't long before some of these new settlers came to visit their Algonquin neighbours, bearing gifts of food and tools in exchange for tanned hides and moccasins, and especially for the Anishinàbe snowshoes.

The new settlement became a village, with people building houses on both sides of the river. They had named their little village, Kitegewaki, or Farmland. Most of the newly arrived people were farmers, or would be as soon as the land was cleared. A store was built along the east bank of the Àndeg Zibi. It was only a matter of time before Anishinàbe customers walked through its doors. They came to trade their winter stock of furs for items that, until then, were available only at the trading post many paddling days south. Now, they purchased rifles and tents, heavy wool blankets, and axes as well as files to keep the blades sharp, and all of these were just a short canoe trip from their homes.

One item had changed the lives of many of the younger men in the Ándeg Zibi community. It was not something that could be purchased at the store in Kitigewaki. As a rule, no one ever paid for this particular item. Most often it began as a gift from one person to another. Like everything else that occurred there, this ritual was increasingly repeated from one year to the next. One day, no one remembers when, one of the white settlers visited the community carrying a furry bundle in his arms, a puppy, which he offered as a gift to one of the children. The puppy grew up, strong and friendly, and soon parents of other children went looking for similar puppies in the village of Kitigewaki. In no time at all, the community was host to a large number of these furry animals that the white settlers referred to as wolf dogs. They were, in fact, Alaskan Malamutes, the same breed of dog that their Anishinàbe cousins used for travelling across the barren ice fields. Even though change was normally slow in coming to the Àndeg Zibi community, the transition from men hauling toboggans to riding a basket sled pulled by a team of Alaskan Malamutes was a fairly rapid one. The young men had seen some of the white trappers with their dogs in harness, hauling supplies to their winter camps. The leather harness, its thick round collar stuffed with deer hair, was simple enough to put together. There were expert snowshoe men in the community who easily copied the basket sleds for any man who wanted one.

Another major change occurred among the Àndeg Zibi Anishinàbek. This change affected all but the eldest members of the community who had no interest whatsoever in learning the language of the white settlers. Before a second generation of Anishinàbe sled-dog handlers came to be, the white settlers of Kitigewaki bestowed upon the lovely, gentle Àndeg

Zibi, the name, Crow River. Most people referred to the river as, simply, the Crow. It was not completely disrespectful. After all, Àndeg Zibi is "Crow River" in the language of the Algonquin people

The elders of the community continued to snow-shoe quietly westward to set traps and snares for both meat and furs. But most of the trapping was done further north. These trappers were the younger men and women of the community who travelled by dog team. Sometimes, two or more couples would team up on their trap lines, sharing a canvas tent and equipment and returning to the community after short stays in the bush.

Armand and Tina Towahibì were very successful trappers. Armand was especially well known for his ability as a sled-dog trainer. He and Tina had a team of Malamutes that were not only strong brutes but extremely fast as well. Armand's best friend, Johnny Kinòje, had raised a team with the same bloodline as Armand's dogs. In fact, his first two puppies came from Armand's lead dog, Meetik.

Armand and Tina always trapped together. They did everything together. Sometimes, they invited their good friends, Johnny Kinòje and his wife Evangeline, to join them on the trail as their trap lines were close to one another. They travelled on the Crow, each going to their respective trap lines and, at day's end, they met back at the prospector tent they had set up previously, somewhere between their two lines.

Soon after their arrival at the camp, Armand and Johnny went about cutting and splitting firewood. Then the dogs were fed. Tina and Evangeline feathered balsam branches for the camp bed and, after, they prepared supper on a tin stove. During supper, they talked about the day's work, how well the dogs had behaved or, if not, what had to be done to change things. Johnny told some of his famous stories. He was known as the best storyteller in the whole community. All four stretched out on the canvas tarpaulin covering the balsam boughs, listening to Johnny's story and drinking a last cup of tea. And then, it was time; Armand lowered the wick on the oil lamp as the others quickly slipped into their sleeping bags. On a clear night, the light from the stars created a soft glow inside the tent, a shade of darkness seen in no other place. There were puffing sounds coming from the tin stove, a last piece of wood thrown onto the fire before they turned in for the night. They might hear the occasional ring of metal chain as one of the Malamutes stood up to stretch or change positions in its sleeping place on the stake chain. A dog might yawn or more than likely, curl its lips back to expose threatening fangs and growl a warning to its nearest neighbours. When the two couples camped together, there were fourteen Malamutes on the stake line. This made for a very long chain stretched between two trees. It also created a situation that could lead to trouble, especially if Meetik or any of the other female dogs happened to be in a loving way. On very cold nights, they could hear the poplar trunks cracking and the river ice expanding and producing the haunting sounds that draw the attention of even the most experienced camper.

* * *

One morning, Johnny and Evangeline said good-bye to her mother and they joined Armand and Tina in the dog yard behind their cabin. All four worked quickly, preparing for another trip north on the Crow. It would probably be their last trip of the season. It had been a good year and, already, they had a lot of quality furs. This would be their last camping trip before spring breakup. Both couples were looking forward to being together in the bush. The dogs were in excellent shape, having covered many miles on the trap lines and the frozen Crow River.

On this particular night, the sun had set well below the spruce and pine and the undulating blackness of the mountains to the west. It was dark but when there was a break in the clouds, the flat, snow-covered Àndeg Zibi was suddenly lit up by a full moon and soft shadows appeared along its shores. Just above the western shoreline, two human figures sat silhouetted before a fire. The dry, dead spruce cracked and spewed parts of itself into the night beyond. The man and the woman sat on their snow-shoes in the snow with their feet stretched out towards the fire.

"What will we do?" the woman said.

"Eat," the man answered.

"I mean, after."

The man stirred stew in a large metal cup. He looked at the woman.

"Eat," he said. "Tomorrow, we head back."

"But the others!" the woman sobbed.

The man ate from his cup with a spoon. When he had finished, he rinsed the cup with snow and poured tea into it from a blackened tea pail sitting next to the fire. The woman wiped a hand across her nose. She had stopped crying. She picked up her cup and spoon and began to eat.

"It's cold," she said.

"Put it back in the pot."

The woman lifted the cover off the pot. Steam arose from within it. She emptied the stew from her cup into the pot and moved the pot closer to the fire.

"Here," the man said. He held the tea pail by its wire handle and poured tea into her cup.

It was a quiet night. Only the fire made a sound. Sometimes, they heard a poplar cracking.

"Do you think we have enough wood?"

"Don't worry about the wood. There's plenty of wood."

"What if we fall asleep? The fire will go out."

"Yes."

"What then?"

"Nothing."

"What do you mean, nothing? Don't you worry about anything, Armand?"

"No."

The man reached into a canvas bag. He did not look into the bag but felt around inside it as he stared towards the fire.

"Here, soak these," he said.

The dried dates that were hard from the cold softened in the hot tea. The woman chewed the dates and turned her head away from the smoke of the fire blowing her way. When she looked back towards the fire, the man was gone.

"Armand?" she called.

The man did not answer but she could hear the short lengths of chain as the dogs stood up and tried pulling away from the confines of the stake line. Often, she had watched Armand checking the dogs before going to bed. There was a rapport between Armand and his seven Malamutes and the extreme contrasts in the dogs had always intrigued her; the loving canine rubbing up against the man as he stroked it caressingly and, then, the bared threatening fangs as Armand moved on to the next dog on the line. Seven Malamutes, all with tails curved above their backs, vying for the man's attention, to respond affectionately to his touch or to snarl and tear at fur and flesh of their teammates on the line.

Armand stayed a little longer caressing Meetik with his bared hand. When he finished, he turned his back on the dogs and urinated on the snow. It had been a long day. Armand was tired. Both Armand and Tina were tired. It was going to be a very cold night and they were tired; that alone could be dangerous.

"Finished?"

"Yes," she replied.

Tina scraped at the bottom of her cup with the spoon. The juice from the stew had frozen around the inside of the cup.

Armand threw two large chunks of wood onto the fire. He walked past the fire and disappeared into the darkness. The two new chunks ignited together and, in the soft light that they spread out over the snow, Tina could see Armand and the sled and each dog's harness spread out on the trail just as they had left them. Armand bent over the sled. He removed the elastic ties and peeled back the canvas tarpaulin.

"Tina, come here," he said.

The woman stood up and walked through the deep snow to the sled. She was tired and just lifting her feet out of the deep snow to walk had winded her. Armand handed her one edge of a folded groundsheet and motioned that he wanted her to spread it out on the snow. Onto this canvas sheet, they began to unload the contents of the sled; canvas bags of food, kitchen utensils, oil lamp and fuel, sleeping bag, shovel blade and handle. He slipped the shovel handle into its blade, inserted the holding pin, and handed the shovel to the woman.

"Here," he said. "Make a hole just big enough."

Tina understood. They had done this before, in spring, when the evenings were only cool and they had been too tired, or too late to set up a tent. Now, there was no tent. They had been using Johnny's tent on this trip. The tent and stove had been packed in Johnny's sled.

Armand walked ahead of her towards the fire. He picked up the axe and disappeared into the thick evergreen forest. Tina began to shovel. The snow came out in solid chunks and she piled them close around the hole. As she worked, the ring of Armand's axe came through the darkness to her. The hole was finished when Armand returned. He dumped the load of balsam boughs by the hole and walked back into the bush. He worked steadily, cutting branches in the dark and thinking of nothing but what he had to do next. That was all there was. He had been caught like this before. Do one thing at a time, in its time, then the next thing when its time comes.

Tina had done a good job. The branches were well feathered, from the front of the hole nearest to the fire towards the back. The aroma of crushed balsam boughs mingled with the smoke from the fire and together they gave the hole some semblance of a place of comfort and security. Armand dropped his second load of branches by the hole and Tina immediately began removing the softer green branches from the woody stems. This last bundle was enough to complete the balsam bed.

Armand returned to the sled. He removed the canvas tarpaulin, the one that had covered all of their supplies in the sled, and dragged it across the snow to the fire.

"Here," he said, handing Tina two points of the tarpaulin.

Tina stood with her back to the fire. She held her arms outstretched, keeping the tarpaulin open. Armand stood above and behind the hole. He pulled the tarpaulin taut and, together, they let it drop to the bed of branches. The tarp was doubled. After they had placed it such that it overlapped the back wall of the snow hole and its folded end covered the foot of the balsam bed, Armand peeled one layer forward, towards the fire. He handed it to Tina who pulled the section towards herself and folded it neatly across the opening of the hole. This part would be used later, to keep frost from forming on the sleeping bag.

Armand returned to the sled. He turned it over, leaving the metal-shod runners facing upwards. He gathered up the long string of dog harnesses and placed them in a pile between the runners. That way they were less likely to be torn to bits should one of the dogs escape from the stake line during the night. He returned to the fire carrying a long, slender bag. He opened the bag and began pulling out the green, down-filled sleeping bag that he tossed onto the tarpaulin.

"There," he said when he had finished. "Be sure to shake up the feathers."

Armand folded the empty bag over the handle of the shovel that stood upright in the snow. It was important that everything should be in its place, always in its proper place, and this had nothing to do with neatness, or tidiness, or any of a multitude of obsessions of any kind. To Armand and any of the people who had survived extremely cold nights in the bush, being able to find things, quickly and without searching, could often mean the difference between staying alive and freezing to death.

Tina stretched the sleeping bag to its full length, shaking the downy fill to life. She folded the tarp over the sleeping bag and made a neat fold just at the opening of the bag.

Armand removed his parka and stuffed it into the sleeping bag sack. He motioned to Tina to do the same. He worked quickly, stuffing her parka into the sack. He tied the bag shut and tossed it to the woman. She peeled back the upper portion of the sleeping bag and put the stuffed sack, now a pillow, into its place. She sat on the tarp, tapped her feet together sharply to remove any snow, and slipped inside the sleeping bag.

The man threw two more chunks of wood onto the fire. He sat on the tarp, next to the woman, tapped his feet together, and slipped into the sleeping bag. He reached forward and pulled the tarp up to their chins.

The wood cracked and the flames danced with the shadows of the forest. It was quiet and cold, very cold. The man and the woman lay next to each other in the sleeping bag with only their faces showing and both of them wearing heavily knitted wool toques. Their breath came in slow, rhythmic clouds of steam, and they were warmed by each other's body heat that stayed inside with them. Silently, they watched the fire slowly dying and waited for sleep to come.

But sleep would not come. The things that had to be done, each in its own time, were done now. It was very cold but everything had been taken care of. Now, they were safe. The body was safe and warm. There was only the mind to care for, to comfort and prepare for what was to come.

"Armand?" the woman whispered. She did not want to wake him if he was sleeping.

"Yes," he answered.

The woman rolled onto her side and rested her head on his chest.

"Armand, what will we do?"

"I don't know."

"It's not our fault, is it?"

"It's nobody's fault. It was the ice, that's all."

The woman began to cry. She held onto him and cried with her head on his chest. The man wrapped his arms over her back and held her to him. He looked up through the branches of the tall white pine above them. He could see the stars through the spaces between the branches, clear and bright as they were the previous night and so they would be tomorrow night and a thousand, thousand nights after. Only the clouds could trick you into believing that they were not always there. In two months, maybe less, the ice would be gone and the tracks of the runners and the jagged hole where Evangeline and Johnny and their seven Malamutes went through would also have disappeared. There would only be waves crossing where they had gone down. No one could tell, just looking there, that two people's lives had ended on the Crow. Two wonderful, good, happy friends and their seven Malamutes struggling in their harnesses right up to the end, the leader's paws still fighting the thin ice as the weight of the sled, and Johnny and Evangeline, dragged them under.

Armand tried not to think about it, but it was too clear. Yes, so very clear. He could still hear the whines of the dogs, and Evangeline coughing up water the last time he saw her face.

"Tina," he said. "Stop, Tina. It won't help."

He could feel the woman's head nodding in agreement. Still, she continued to cry softly. At last, the crying stopped but there was a tremor to her breathing. Armand avoided speaking to her. He rubbed the back of her shoulders and waited. She would be exhausted soon and with exhaustion would come calm and, perhaps, sleep. Not peaceful sleep, but tired, disturbing excursions of the mind, a time of unconsciousness to pass away time. He would not sleep. He knew that. He would be awake in the night, with the stars, and he would go over it all in his mind and how he would do each thing in its turn. After he had notified the Mounties at Kitigewaki, and fed the dogs, he would walk up the path to the old house where Evangeline and Johnny had lived with her mother. He would tell her what a fine trip it had been going over Potato Mountain and along the Crow, and how sad it was that, just two days from home, the ice was bad in one place, the place where Evangeline and Johnny went down. She was an old woman who knew plenty about sled dogs. She would become angry, and she would scream that no good leader would walk on bad ice. She would curse Kayak, Johnny's lead dog, and all of his predecessors and all of his descendants that might have been. Finally, she would sit down, swaying back and forth and crying that mournful lament for the dead.

Armand felt Tina's warmness on his chest. He caressed her shoulders, and her neck, and he held her to him. She was a strong woman. When many days had passed and she had accepted and adjusted to her great loss, that Evangeline and Johnny were no more, she would be strong. He would need her in the night, for he would not sleep, he would not easily adjust, and he would need her to hold him close to her, to remind him always, that she was still with him. He would sell the team. They were good mutts, all of them, and he knew several men who would be willing to take Meetik, and he knew they would treat her well. There would be no more trips to the trap line, at least not on the Crow. In summer, of course, they would fish and they would go for moose in the fall. But his canoe would never glide over that spot on the Crow, even if it was the best, deepest place for bass.

The woman stirred. She drew closer and the warmth of their bodies joined together through the layers of heavy clothing.

"Armand?" she said.

"Enhenh."

"Aren't you tired? You must be so tired."

"No, I'm all right."

"You want me to get off? Maybe you'll sleep then."

"No, Tina. Stay."

The dying embers of the fire snapped in the cold silence of the night. A wind had begun to blow and whistle through the needles of the pine. Still, they heard it. Both Tina and Armand lifted their heads and listened to the mournful lament of a lone grey wolf paying tribute to its seven cousins who would never pad trails on the Crow again. Now, only their spirits would lope along the frozen Àndeg Zibi, like the spirits of the elders who paddle this great river as they did so many generations past.

The Fiat

As he came over the top of the hill, following the tire tracks in the snow, he saw her. That is to say, he saw a great bundle of fur leaning against a lamppost at the intersection. The hydro pole across the highway was leaning over at a steep angle and steam was rising from a deep V notched into the front of her car.

Henri began to slow down, shifting from fourth to third, to second, and only then did he dare to touch the brake pedal. Immediately, the car swerved from one side to another with each correction of the steering wheel. Finally it stopped, three feet from the mass of fur clinging to the lamppost.

"Need a hand?" Henri called from the car. He wasn't sure if there was life beneath the fur. Perhaps someone had left it there after the accident. There were no other tracks but those leading from the broken hydro pole. Henri tried again, calling from the open window of his little Fiat, the motor idling and he, tapping the accelerator occasionally to keep the motor from dying. "You need a hand there?"

"Well, well, my saviour, my knight in shining armour," the woman's voice became progressively higher pitched as the words rolled out. "Got anything to drink, my boy?"

That's all I need, he thought, a drunken woman driver and an all-night snowstorm. And it's Christmas Eve for Christ's sake. I can't just leave her. These thoughts crossed his mind, not necessarily in that order.

"Can I give you a lift somewhere?" Henri replied. He purposely avoided the question about the booze. He just hated telling a drunk he had no booze. It was like being in a confessional box and telling the priest you have no sins. He added, "Are you okay?"

"Me? Shit-a goddamn! There's nothing wrong with me. I'm a little late for the party. But that's all right. I'll make it."

"What about the car?"

"Screw the car. I don't really give a good goddamn about the car. Made it this far didn't I?"

"Yeah, well. Anyone call the cops? It might be a long wait. Roads are pretty bad. You can get in with me while you're waiting."

Fur Coat stood up, pushing herself away from the lamppost as she took two very big steps towards the Fiat. She leaned over to speak to Henri, the folds of her greatcoat opening and her hands resting on the roof of the little car.

"Listen to me, sonny boy," she began. "If you think I'm going to hang around this stinking hole waiting for some smart-ass cop to read me my rights and tell me exactly how much alcohol I've got floating in my veins, and all of this while my friends are whooping it up in some cozy lodge north of here. Look at me, sonny. Is it written anywhere on my face, eh? Is 'stupid' written anywhere on this face of mine, eh? So, let me get my presents out of that piece of junk over there. You got room on the back seat, or maybe in the trunk?"

Henri watched the woman as she shuffled through the snow to the other side of the highway. She opened the trunk and pulled out a department store bag full of gifts, all wrapped in Christmas paper and tied with large red bows. She didn't close the trunk lid and it began to fill with snow.

"Going to close the trunk?" Henri inquired. He helped her place the presents on the back seat, alongside his three tiny presents wrapped in plain brown paper.

"Naah," she said. "The wreck's still on warranty. They'll probably write it off anyway. So, where you headed, sonny?"

Before Henri could answer, the woman began to twist and slide her body and her enormous fur coat into the tiny bucket seat. Henri had to step out of the car and over to the passenger side to close the door behind her.

"North," he said. "About another eighty miles or so."

"Good, good," she said. "Name's Marie-Andrée Simard-Bellevue. Just call me Betsy. What's your name, sonny?"

"Henri. Henri Lauzon."

"Now that's a good Irish name, Henri Lauzon. Tell me something, Henri. What's all that snow doing piled up on the hood?"

"There's no hood. It got lost a couple of years ago. Snow's been piling up inside."

The woman searched in her handbag, tossing articles around inside until she found her cigarettes. Then she began a search again, looking for matches. Henri shifted into gear and slowly drove out onto the road, first, second, and then third gear. He needed more speed for fourth.

"Never thought a motor could work in snow like that," she said, her hand searching deep inside the handbag. "Got a match?"

"Motor's in the back. Up there's the trunk." Henri handed the woman a small box of wooden matches. He downshifted, slowing down by the roadside.

"What's up, Henri?" she looked at him.

"Go ahead, light up," he said. "There're cracks in the doors. Wind comes through pretty strong when we're moving."

The woman laughed, holding the cigarette between her teeth as she tightened the fur around her neck and head. She looked over at Henri who was driving with his mitts on.

"How about the door," she said, "is it okay to lean against it?"

"Your door's okay." Henri checked the seat belt to make sure his was looped around the door handle.

"It's my door that's bad: if I turn to the right too fast, door kind of opens."

"Hee, hee, hee! Christ, wait 'til I tell them down at the office." The woman laughed, her head bent low, almost on her knees, and holding her cigarette high above her head.

She inhaled deeply and then, out it came, through both nostrils and bellowing out between the thick red lines of her lips. Scary, that was all Henri could think. And he prayed for guidance on the road. Stuck in this little Fiat, somewhere in a snow bank with fur coat for company was a little more than he could take. Less than two miles north of the accident, he spotted the taillights of a car travelling up ahead. At last, tracks that he could follow. Now he didn't have to guess where the road was. Earlier, when he had locked up his cabin and eased out onto the highway, the driving snow was just too much for his aging windshield wipers. He suddenly found himself facing a brick building. He had entered someone's driveway. He could see children looking at him from the living room window.

"So, Henri," Fur Coat said cheerfully, as if everything was now settled and they were safely on their way. "Tell me about yourself. Are you a working lad?"

"No, not exactly. I'm a student at the university, in the Capital."

"I see. One of them starving student types, eh? I almost did that, go to university, that is. So, how do you manage, with a car and everything?"

Henri had to turn to look at her. He was wearing his parka hood and his vision was limited to straight ahead. He downshifted again, from fourth to third, to second, and slowly pushed down on the brake pedal as he pulled over to the side of the road.

"Now what?" the woman looked at him.

"Want to have a smoke."

"Can't you drive and smoke at the same time? Here, I'll light it for you with mine."

"It's kind of hard with mitts."

Henri removed the heavy, lined mitts and placed them between himself and Fur Coat. He pulled out a cigarette from his shirt pocket and, holding his hand cupped around the match, lit up and inhaled deeply, tapping the accelerator lightly as he stretched.

"My neighbour gave me the car. He's a professor at the university. One day, he was driving along the freeway and the hood opened and flew over the top of the car. He didn't look back. He just kept right on driving. The next day, he went out and bought himself a brand new car."

"So that's how you got a car. Well, good for him. I suppose that he could easily have sold it for a good price."

"I'm not so sure. It's got a few bugs, like the door I told you about. And the missing hood, of course. Starting it is something else. My neighbour, the professor, gets up a half-hour earlier every morning just to see me start the thing. I think he gets a kick out of that."

Henri scraped at the windshield that was starting to freeze up inside. He opened the window a bit on his side but the breeze in the car didn't change at all.

"I tried everything," Henri went on. "During the winter, I tried an electric blanket around the battery, a two hundred watt light bulb resting on the motor block, and a block heater, of course. I even tried spraying the carburetor intake with ether. The explosion is really something. Every morning, I check that all the wires are in place, that the connections to the battery are good and tight, and then, the big moment, when I turn the key. Sometimes, there's a burring sound but, more often than not, silence, broken only by the sound of my neighbour laughing so hard I can hear him through the double windows of his house."

Henri opened the window wider and flicked his cigarette out onto the snow. He raised the window, placed the parka hood over his head, put his mitts on and shifted into gear.

"Then what?" Fur Coat lit up another cigarette. "What do you do then?"

"Well, you see, my cabin's on a little bit of a hill. So I put the car in neutral and push it, with the door open, and when I figure that I've got enough speed, I jump in, shift into third and pop the clutch. That usually works."

"But in town," Fur Coat insisted. "Surely there's no hill in the university parking lot."

"Carry booster cables, and a chain."

"Yeah, I suppose." Fur Coat was at a loss for words. She turned to look at him. "You know, sonny, I really envy you. You're as poor as rat shit and having the time of your life. I really admire you for that."

Now it was Henri's time to be at a loss for words. He would have been even more perplexed had he seen the tears that slid slowly down her cheeks. Fur Coat dug into her large handbag and withdrew a handful of tissues. She blew her nose, and dabbed lightly beneath each eye.

"So tell me, Henri," she said, at last, "What's this town you're going to? Is that home?"

"It's where I was born. The town is called Valcourt, another forty miles on this highway, and then another thirty miles on the main route north. So, where are you headed?"

"Well, I'm not really sure. It's some kind of tourist club. It's on a large lake next to a village called Sainte-Anne du Lac. Ever hear of it?"

"Sure," Henri said. He knew exactly where she was going. The village was about ten miles off the main highway and the club, L'Anse du Poisson Blanc, was another two or three miles west of the village. "I know exactly where you're going."

There was suddenly a certain silence in the car, the kind of silence that allows you to hear all the sounds that the motor is not supposed to be making, the tiny wipers screeching across the frozen windshield, the heater motor doing its best even though the bushings have long ago worn through.

It was a time of silence that Fur Coat felt she could not impose upon, a time when Henri thought about how he just could not abandon her on the highway, in the middle of a snowstorm. The road from the village to the club might not be ploughed. He might run out of gas. Could she walk that far, with the presents and that great big coat?

"Madame," Henri began.

"Betsy," she interrupted him.

"Betsy," Henri began again. "I'm not sure if I can make it to the club but I'll start by getting you to the village. We'll see from there."

"Oh, you're an angel, Henri." Fur Coat giggled and began to fumble in her large handbag once again. She slipped out a short, flat bottle. She unscrewed the cap and offered the bottle to Henri.

Henri shook his head, no. "Thanks anyway," he said.

"Aw, come on, it's Christmas," Fur Coat sang the words. "You sure, Henri?"

Henri glanced to his right and, in the darkness of the car—the dash lights no longer gave off any light—, he could see Fur Coat's head tilted back and her left elbow sticking out at him as she held the bottle to her lips.

Henri downshifted when he saw the sign, "Sainte-Anne du Lac 15 km." Slowly, and in a wide turn, he left the main highway and moved forward along the narrow stretch of road. There were no tire tracks in the snow. He was careful not to accelerate too brusquely, not to cause his rear tires to spin, although he had real snow tires on all four wheels. These tires were the only part of the car that was not old and worn out. But this was deep snow. The car came from Italy, so the floorboards were only inches above the snow. Henri really wasn't sure they could make it.

As they approached the sign that said, "Bienvenue à Sainte-Anne du Lac," Fur Coat grew excited. She lowered the sun visor and tried to see herself in the tiny mirror. She pumped at her hair with the fingers of both hands and lifted the back of her hair with open palms. She fished into the handbag and soon was spreading lipstick over what was already there.

"It's so good of you, Henri," she said, trying to see out through the frozen-over window. I don't know what I would have done without your help. You must be my guardian angel."

Henri slowed down and finally came to a full stop between the *dépanneur* and the hotel. There were no lights on in either building. It was Christmas Eve after all. His little spring-wound pocket watch said eleven thirty. This was probably correct, plus or minus five minutes or so. In any case, he would not be home for at least another hour. He would be too late for midnight mass but he might arrive in time for the *réveillon*, the Christmas Eve party. That is, if they didn't get stuck or run out of gas, or both. The gas gauge in the Fiat didn't work so he wasn't sure what their chances were. But he had decided: he could not leave her there, between the closed *dépanneur* and the hotel at this hour of the night on Christmas Eve.

"Well, here goes," Henri said to no one in particular.

"I'll drink to that!" Fur Coat muttered aloud. It sounded almost like a prayer. She tilted the bottle back and held it there until it was empty. "I'll never forget what you're doing for me, Henri. I think that this is the best Christmas Eve in my whole life."

Once again, there was a scramble for her handbag and her blowing her nose and dabbing lightly beneath her eyes. This time, Henri turned to look at her. He turned away just as quickly and tightened his mitts around the steering wheel. He found it difficult seeing Fur Coat with tears in her eyes. And it would have been even more difficult had he known that he was the cause of her tears. Henri cleared his throat and concentrated on the road ahead. There would be time for talk later.

Although no tracks were visible on the road and the snow was deep, it was not slippery and Henri could feel the tires gripping the snow well and pulling them along. He drove slowly and he could hear the engine whining as he kept the car in low gear and they moved forward easily, with no sudden movements, going along the middle of the road with the dark green of the pines on both sides of them and snowflakes falling in front of the tiny headlights. They were going to make it. He was sure of that now and he began to relax. He removed the parka hood from his head and he lightened his grip on the steering wheel. He removed one mitt and took out a cigarette from his shirt pocket.

"Would you mind?" he said, handing the cigarette to Fur Coat.

"For you, Henri, anything." she said. Fur Coat took the cigarette and lit it, and handed it back to Henri. She leaned over then and rubbed his back and slid her hand beneath the curls along his neck. "Oh, if I was a younger woman, Henri."

Henri drove with one mitt on the steering wheel. Fur Coat wasn't so scary any more and he wondered what she must have been like twenty years ago. He had never met a woman quite like her.

As they came around a sharp bend in the road, the lighted clubhouse appeared before them. It was an enormous log structure with tall narrow windows and a great stone chimney rising out of the centre of the roof. Through the windows he could see the women in their colourful dresses and the men in jackets gathered around the open fireplace. Everyone looked warm and happy. Henri stepped out of the car. He went around to the passenger side and helped Fur Coat out of the bucket seat. He leaned inside, to the back seat, and pulled out the shopping bag with all of her Christmas gifts.

"Here you go, Betsy." Henri handed her the shopping bag. "It's been great."

"Hey, hold on a minute there. You're not getting off that easy. You've got to come in and have a drink with me. We can warm up by the fire. You can see the fire from here. See?"

"Yes, I see. But I really have to go. There are people waiting for me: my parents, my sister Karine and her new boyfriend, and my brother Albert. Thanks just the same."

"Are you sure?"

"Yep, I really have to go."

He wanted to say more, silly things like, I think I'm going to miss you.

"Well, so long Betsy. Merry Christmas," was all he could say.

"Henri, I'm so happy to have met you." Fur Coat leaned forward and kissed him on the mouth. "I won't forget you, ever."

Fur Coat left him then, walking up the steps to the lodge, carrying the shopping bag with her presents with one hand and hanging onto the railing with the other. Upon reaching the veranda, she turned to wave to Henri. All she could see were the taillights of the little Fiat going around the bend in the road.

The rest of the trip home was a lonely one. Henri kept repeating in his mind the conversation he and Fur Coat had shared on their way to the tourist lodge. It wasn't much perhaps but for Henri it had become something special. Now he was alone again and he guessed that their short time together was probably the furthest thing on her mind at that very moment. He was just another event in her life, an event that allowed her to partake in another event, which could possibly lead to another.

But Henri had been wrong about Fur Coat. She had not forgotten him. While he struggled to keep the little Fiat from sliding off the road, Fur Coat leaned against the large stone fireplace, drink in hand and surrounded by an attentive group as she described in great detail her encounter with the hydro-electric pole, her slowly freezing to death as she hung on to a lamppost in the middle of nowhere, and how this young, curly-headed university student came to her rescue. Fur Coat made a point of repeating every word of the conversation she had shared with this young man, much to the enjoyment of her friends. But it was when she described the little Fiat and all of its peculiarities that a screech of laughter arose from the rear of the assembled group. Fur Coat didn't know the young woman, only that her name was Karine. The young woman moved in closer and hugged Fur Coat warmly.

"That curly-headed young man," she said, laughing hysterically, "that was my brother, Henri!"

Conflict

It was a sunny day in July as the women and children lay face up on the hot, black pavement. Less than thirty feet away from them were several tons of coarse gravel laid across the highway. The gravel had been dumped there during the early hours of the morning, hours before the police arrived. The barricade was just north of the prostrate women and children; to the south of these sixty or so bodies was a solid line of squad cars blocking the road. On both sides of the highway and all along its steep banks, the husbands and fathers of the women and children walked to and fro, carrying coloured placards with nasty messages written in black ink.

The patrol cars blocking the south section were polished and shone brightly in the afternoon sun. The cars' radio-telephones had been switched over to their external speakers hidden beneath the hoods of the patrol cars. The volume had been turned up full so that everyone gathered there could hear the coded messages and the radio-repeater return signals, a grim-sounding "Pshhht" at the end of each transmission.

It was the lieutenant's idea. Lieutenant Harold Morrow was his own greatest admirer, perhaps the only one. It was, in his opinion, the best and only method of crowd control, next to bashing their heads in, of course. Fear was the only concept that these people understood. But the lieutenant was subtle. That much could be said of him. He had ordered his men to refrain from drawing their service revolvers. He also told them to leave their batons in the patrol cars. They were to stand by their cars, surveying each and every move. Fear itself would take care of the rest: the constant coded messages blaring from the hidden speakers, the flashing lights of the patrol cars, the persistent feeling of being corralled between the squad cars and the great pile of gravel to the north. The claustrophobic amongst them would be the first to crack.

"Just wait," Lieutenant Morrow spoke out of the corner of his mouth. He looked at the officer standing next to him. "Just wait until the kids start pissing their pants, and crying because they're hungry."

"Yes sir," the officer replied.

Corporal Antoine Binet looked at the women lying on the pavement; some were on closed-cell foam sleeping mats, others lay directly on the tarstone pavement. They didn't look hungry and the children were not crying either. Several men walked among them, offering sandwiches and cold drinks and candy bars to the children. Other men distributed hot tea in Styrofoam cups to the women. The 'fear factor' was not evident here. Were it not for the stringent remarks scribbled on the colourful plac-ards carried by the men, the assembled group reminded Binet more of the festive picnics of his village than a mob of angry protestors. He thought of mentioning these observations to Lieutenant Morrow but he knew better. To declare openly that the lieutenant's idea, his 'fear factor,' was not work-ing would leave him, corporal Binet, latest arrival on the force, liable to night shift duty for the next two or three months. Still, it was odd, they did not seem to be running out of provisions. Someone had even set up a tent kitchen. Already, large cast-iron pots hung over an open fire. Binet could have sworn that the odour drifting his way was that of baked beans. And the atmosphere was almost cheerful, with laughing children playing on the pavement and men waving placards and sharing jokes to pass away the time. There were no signs of fear to be found anywhere.

When the women and their children first began lying on the pavement they did so to disrupt traffic moving along the highway. This was a major thor-oughfare, Highway 555, connecting the northern mining towns with the big cities to the south. It was immediate: as soon as the drivers saw the bodies scattered across the pavement, sixty of them in no particular order, they came to a stop and pulled over to the side of the road to wait. Wait for what? Were they waiting for the women and children to stand up and walk away? That would not be happening. And then there were the men on the steep embankments with placards and angry words. So the line-ups on both sides of the gathering of women and children grew and grew until, by nightfall, it was more than a mile long in either direction. Some of the drivers turned around in the middle of the road and headed back to where they came from. Others slept in their cars with the windows open, while still others left their cars and walked along the line-up, chatting with the drivers.

After the loads of gravel were dumped across the highway, the bodies of the women and children stretched out on the pavement became a symbolic gesture. But a gesture of defiance nonetheless, and one that made the mothers and the children especially proud. They were doing their part.

"Did you notice the kitchen, sir?" Binet said, casually, without looking at the lieutenant. "Where do we stand on campfires along here, sir?"

"I don't give a sweet goddamn about their campfires." The lieutenant looked at his watch. "I've ordered ambulances in from both north and south. They should be here any minute now. That might get the bastards thinking."

"Accidents sir?" Binet looked around for signs.

"Goon squad's coming. Bus should be here in about an hour. Not as if we need them. Christ!"

"We know that, sir," was all Binet dared to say. There were things better left unsaid.

The lieutenant leaned into the patrol car through the open window. When he straightened up, he held a telephone handset, stretching the coiled wire that led to the radio transmitter inside.

"Attention all staff!" the lieutenant smiled at the sound of his own voice coming from the external speakers. "No one enters or leaves the site. The riot squad has been ordered in. ETA, fourteen-thirty hours. Repeat! No one enters or leaves the area."

There was a sudden radio-repeater "Pshhht," and then silence as the lieutenant tossed the handset onto the driver's seat.

"That should stir them up," the lieutenant chuckled.

"Yes sir," Binet responded. He did not agree but he felt obliged somehow to say something. He looked out at the people. They were organized and they were angry. But, most important of all, they believed that they were right. They believed firmly in the righteousness of their cause. This alone, Binet believed, was a staunch adversary to force. The ambulances that the lieutenant had ordered might prove to be more practical than he intended.

The two ambulances arrived at almost the same time. One vehicle was parked along the north side of the gravel barricade while the other ambulance maneuvered in between two patrol cars, turned, and backed in as close as it could to the human barricade, its "Reverse" warning horn blaring loudly over the crowd. The northern ambulance personnel left the highway and walked down into the ditch as they made their way to the patrol cars. One of the two men carried a portable radiophone and both men had stethoscopes draped around their necks. After they had walked past the women and children on the pavement, the two ambulance attendants joined the South ambulance personnel standing next to the patrol cars and all four shook hands vigorously and almost immediately began sharing anecdotes and laughing loudly. The policemen looked at them, sternly. Somehow, and for reasons unknown, the police officers had always felt that they were a cut above these unarmed men in uniforms, these aficionados of blood-strewn highway accidents and brain-scattered suicide events, these almost medics, strutting around emergency rooms as if they were, in fact, part of the emergency staff. Still, the officers were always relieved to see them arrive when things got messy. These unarmed men in uniforms were always there to pick up the pieces and take them away.

To the women lying on the pavement and their men protesting along the steep banks of the highway, these were just more men in uniform. True, these men did not carry guns and more often than not their arrival upon a scene inspired confidence and hope. But today, despite the "Torch and Serpent" and "AMBULANCE" on their shoulder patches, despite the emergency symbols covering the vehicles they drove, they had joined the enemy upon their arrival; they had not remained neutral, they showed no support of any kind. Not even for the children.

At exactly two-thirty in the afternoon, a grey, commercial-size bus arrived. The bus turned crosswise on the highway and stopped there with a loud hiss of its air brakes. The windows of the bus were clouded over in black and for a long time nothing occurred. The door remained closed for at least ten minutes after the driver had shut down the engine.

"Come on, come on!" Lieutenant Morrow murmured. "What the hell's the problem?"

Finally, the door opened and the driver stepped down from the bus. He did not look at the line of patrol cars or the policemen standing by them. The driver opened the storage compartment doors and returned inside the bus. Immediately, men began stepping out of the bus, strongly built men with cropped hair and all wearing bulletproof vests and heavy leather boots. The men, all twenty of them, went directly to the storage compartments and selected their gear: helmets, batons, and shields. The last person to come out of the bus, also strongly built, with short, grey hair, carried a megaphone in one hand.

The arrival of the riot squad had an effect on the people but, much to the disappointment of the lieutenant, the sensation created was one more of interest than of fear. They had never seen a riot squad. Even the women looked up in awe at these handsome, squarely built men.

The lieutenant was to experience a second disappointment. The officer in charge, the grey-haired gentleman with the megaphone, stood before his twenty officers and spoke to them in a casual, supportive manner. The policemen standing by the patrol cars could not hear the words but they sensed that the man was well liked by his men, that they would do absolutely anything he commanded, without a single thought. They stood at attention as he spoke. All eyes looked forward. Only two things were on their minds: what was required of them and when?

Corporal Antoine Binet was impressed as were all of his fellow officers. They did their best to stand at attention by their patrol cars as the "chief" —they had no idea of his name or rank—spoke to his men.

"Binet!" the lieutenant barked. "Go over there and see what he wants us to do."

"Yes sir."

Binet left his position by the patrol car and walked quickly towards the assembled riot squad. He wondered if he should salute when he arrived. As he approached from behind, the man turned to face him, his eyes steady and almost grey like his hair.

"Yes?" he addressed Binet. There was a look about the man that made you want to rehearse what you had to say so as not to waste his time.

"Sir!" was all Binet could say. He said it loudly and plainly and looking straight into the man's eyes. "Lieutenant Morrow sends me, sir. What would you like us to do, sir?"

"What is your name?"

"Corporal Antoine Binet, sir."

"Ok. Tell me, Antoine. Who is in charge here?"

"Lieutenant Morrow, sir."

"No, no. I mean, among the people there, who represents them? Who speaks for them?"

"I'm sorry, sir. I don't know, sir." Binet felt a sudden flush spreading over his face. "But I can find out for you, sir."

"Very good, Antoine. You do that for me." the man said. The man had pursed his lips into a thin smile as he spoke. The young officer interpreted this as approval of sorts, that he was now almost one of them.

Binet returned to his patrol car, walking quickly, with his right hand resting on the holster of his service revolver.

"Well?" Lieutenant Morrow said sharply. "What support does he need? What's his name, anyway?"

"None sir," Binet replied. "I have to go sir."

"Go? Go where?"

"The chief over there, he wants me to find out who's in charge?"

"In charge?" the lieutenant screamed. "I'm in charge here."

"Yes sir. I told him that sir. He wants to know who's in charge of the people, sir."

"The people! Who gives a good goddamn about the people? What's wrong with that man?"

"Yes sir. I'm going now sir. I'll find out who's giving orders among them, sir."

"And report back to me. That's an order Binet."

"Yes sir."

Corporal Binet left the assembled patrol cars and the fuming lieutenant. He stepped carefully over and around the women and children spread out on the pavement. He scanned the banks along both sides of the highway, looking for someone, anyone who looked like he or she might be in charge. The men on the banks raised their placards and stared defiantly at Binet. There was a baby on the pavement who was crying but that was the only sound. As he approached a collection of canvas tents, Binet could hear the wood of the campfire crackling.

"Who's in charge here?" he said to the first person he came to. The young woman had long black hair tied back from her face and left flowing down her back. She wore a plain dress that ended down around her ankles, sky blue with scatterings of white flowers. The woman stirred something in one of the cast iron pots with a long wooden spoon.

"Him, over there," the woman pointed with the spoon. Her dark eyes, almost as black as her hair, stared into Binet's eyes. The police officer, poor fellow, fell instantly under her charm.

Binet walked towards the man. He did his best to walk straight, shoulders squared, a man of purpose and determination. But he felt conquered, completely disabled, and only because of the way she looked at him. He could not imagine how he would have felt if she had actually tried to hit him.

"Corporal Binet," he introduced himself to the man. "I would like your name and what position you hold in this organization."

As Binet withdrew a small notebook and pen from his shirt pocket, the man turned to face him. The man, Binet was quick to observe, had turned only his head and not his whole body and, that alone, put the young policeman on his guard. The man was about forty years old, Binet guessed, but he had the physique of a man of thirty. His dark-skinned face stood out from hair that curved around his cheeks and disappeared behind his back, black with sudden streaks of grey. But his eyes, those deep black eyes, like the woman at the fire, stared into Binet's eyes and it seemed to the young officer that the man could see inside him, could know his very thoughts.

"Why would you want to know my name?" the man turned his body completely around. To Binet, he was suddenly much larger than before.

"The riot squad has arrived. Their chief wants to know who's in charge here." Binet had almost, without thinking, added the word "sir" to the end of his request.

"My name is Isaac. I'm a guide to the people here. What they do is their decision."

Binet was disturbed. The first two sentences uttered by the man called Isaac was all he needed to complete his mission. Now the man, this Isaac, had ruined his simple task. All he needed was a name, a man who speaks for them. That's all the chief had requested. Now this; he was a guide and it was the people who decided. What kind of information was that?

Corporal Binet closed the notebook and placed it and the pen back into his shirt pocket. He nodded politely and turned to leave. The man, smiled at him.

"Have a nice day, my friend," he said.

"Yes, you too." Binet felt sick. Quite possibly the forces of law and order would soon be beating these people's heads in and he was returning the man's good wishes for a nice day.

Binet walked past the woman at the fire. It was beyond his control, he could not go by without looking at her. What was her name? Could he see her when all of this craziness was over?

"You speak to Isaac?" the woman turned to look at him.

"Yes. Thank you very much."

"What is your name?"

"Binet. Antoine Binet. And you?"

"Fawn," she said. She turned then and began stirring the stew in the cast-iron pot. Binet looked around him. There was no one around, no one looking in their direction. He was at a loss as to why she had turned her back on him. There was no reason, at least none that he could see.

"Well?" the lieutenant barked as Binet approached him. "What did you find out? No one's in charge there, I'll bet. Not by the looks of things."

"Yes sir," Binet began. "That's true and not true, sir."

"Now don't you start," the lieutenant snapped. "I just got a call from headquarters. The goons and their chief over there are in charge now. Something political, I don't know. Headquarters are talking something about a white-glove treatment, who knows? So, Binet, get over there with your information and get right back here. We're not part of that squad or anything else that happens here."

"Yes sir. Right away, sir."

The corporal walked, almost ran, across the stretch of highway that separated the patrol cars from the riot squad standing by the bus.

"And so, Antoine," the chief greeted Binet. "What's the word from the people?"

"His name is Isaac, sir. No last name. He claims to be only a guide. The people do as they chose. Sorry sir. That is all the information I could get. There is one other thing, though."

"Yes?"

"Well, sir, I can't be absolutely sure but I did see a trail leading back into the bush and I saw one of those four-wheelers arriving, loaded down with food."

Binet had not mentioned this bit of information to the lieutenant. He had saved it for the chief, a man he was already considering as his superior officer.

"Very good, Antoine. You've done excellent work, my man. Thank you very much."

"Thank you, sir. Will there be anything else sir?"

"No, that will be all for now. We'll call for you if we need you, Antoine."

"Yes sir."

Binet marched back to the patrol car a new man, an assistant to the riot squad. The lieutenant was sitting in the patrol car, next to the driver's seat. Binet walked up to the open window of the patrol car.

"Well?" the lieutenant said.

"Relayed the information, sir. Guess it's up to them now, sir."

"Them? Who are you talking about, corporal?"

"The people, sir. It's up to them, now, how the riot squad will act. I hope that they can come to some agreement. Don't you, sir?"

"I don't give a damn, one way or the other. All I want is for the situation to be over and done with so we can get the hell out of here."

"Yes sir."

Corporal Binet backed away from the patrol car and looked over its top to the enormous bus parked at a right angle to the road.

"It's starting, sir," he said.

The lieutenant turned to look out towards the bus. The twenty members of the squad had lined up and their chief was speaking to them. Suddenly, all twenty began to march in single file, beating their shields in time with their batons as they made their way towards the women and children lying on the pavement. Their chief followed behind, carrying the megaphone in one hand.

The twenty men formed two parallel lines alongside the women and children. Some of the children had been frightened by the sounds of batons striking the transparent shields and they were crying in their mother's arms.

The chief arrived and stood in front of his men. He stood with his back to them as he raised the megaphone up to face level and spoke into the microphone.

"My name is Corbeil. Jean-Louis Corbeil. I am in charge of the men you see behind me. We do not wish you any harm. Our job is a simple one. This highway must be cleared of all obstruction. To begin with, all of the women and children must leave the pavement. If, in five minutes, the road is not clear of people, we will move them out."

As the chief lowered the megaphone, the twenty men behind him began beating their shields with a steady rhythm. The chief glanced at his watch. Suddenly, a man on the far bank, on the same side as the kitchen, stood boldly staring across at the riot squad as he held a chainsaw above his head with one hand, racing the engine repeatedly. This was his response to the riot squad's threats.

Binet did not recognize the man with the chainsaw. It was not Isaac, he was sure of that. The corporal felt sick to his stomach. There were babies on the pavement. Some of the women were pregnant.

"Sir," Binet faced the lieutenant.

"What?"

"We've got to do something, sir. We can't let them go in there with the women and kids."

"Why not? Listen to me, corporal," the lieutenant spoke from the corner of his mouth. "These people started all this and the squad will finish it. It's as simple as that. Stay out of it, Binet. That's an order."

Binet did not answer. The lieutenant looked up when the customary "yes sir" did not reach his ears. Binet was not there. All the lieutenant could see was the young man's back as he ran towards the chief, skipping around the reclined women's bodies and stepping over the smaller children.

As he walked up to the chief, two of his men stepped out of the line-up and stood between their leader and this young, intruding police officer. They held their batons at the ready and waited nervously for the command to attack.

"Antoine," the chief said, in a dull, flat voice. "What do you want?"

"Forgive me, sir," Binet began, looking between the two shields as he spoke to the man. "I spoke to their leader, as you know. Would you please hold off while I speak to him again?"

The chief moved forward. He spoke to the two men standing guard between Binet and himself. The two lowered their batons and returned to the line-up.

"Listen to me, Antoine," the chief began. "You really took a chance running over here like this, even if you are in uniform. My men would easily kill a man just to protect me. So be careful of your moves, Antoine. Now, what is it that you want from me?"

Binet looked at the man. He looked directly into the grey eyes before he spoke. He was not afraid. And he didn't care what Lieutenant Morrow would do to him when this was over. In less than an hour, after being present at what he considered to be the development of a major confrontation and more than a possible blood bath, Binet felt his life take on a whole new meaning. He was terrified of what he was certain would occur in a matter of minutes while, at the same time, he was excited at the direction his life was taking.

"I would like your permission, sir," Binet said clearly. "I would like your permission to go over there and speak to this man Isaac. I would like to bring him over here to speak to you, sir."

"I hope you realize the trouble that you could be getting yourself into, Antoine. And we would not be in a position to help you. Our task has been set for us."

"Yes sir. I'm aware of the situation, sir."

The chief looked at his watch. He turned to his men, all twenty of them ready for action. He turned again to stare at this young police officer, standing there with only hope in his eyes.

"Okay Antoine. Five minutes. That's all I can give you."

"Yes sir. Thank you, sir."

Binet's gaze turned to the men with the batons and shields and then to the men standing on the bank behind them. These men had lowered their placards and waited in silence for the action to begin. Binet pulled at the belt that encircled his waist. He released the duty belt from its buckle and let the collection of gear fall to the ground; pepper spray, handcuffs, the walkie-talkie with its external microphone that had been clipped to his shirt collar, the empty loop that was reserved for the baton, and, finally, his service revolver and a small ammunition pouch. These he had let fall to the pavement with a dull thud. He felt naked and alone as he walked across the road to the kitchen tent and the campfire that was still burning. As he approached the campfire, he saw Isaac waiting for him.

"Isaac," Binet greeted the man.

The man did not answer. He stood by the fire and looked at the young police officer, still in uniform but without the usual tools of his trade. The man suddenly raised a tightly formed fist high above his head. The man's eyes were closed. All Binet could hear was the wood burning in the fire and, from behind him, the chief's men beating their shields with the batons. At last, after more than a minute had passed, Isaac opened his eyes. He turned to the fire and, opening his left hand, released the tobacco into the flames. He turned to face Binet.

"Why have you come?" he said, barely audible over the crackling of the wood fire.

"I'm afraid," Binet answered. He was surprised at his own words. They seemed to come out of his mouth before he even had time to think of them.

The man Isaac stared back at Binet, and as he did so his face softened and the beginning of a smile formed on his lips.

"I'm afraid," Binet repeated. "I'm afraid of what will happen here. I have some understanding of why you people are here but I'm sure that the chief Corbeil over there hasn't the faintest idea of what it's all about. He's been given orders to clear out the road and that's what he'll do. His men are dedicated. They'll do anything for him without question. Those men are trained to do exactly what he tells them to do. For this, Isaac, I'm afraid."

"What do you want from me?" the almost smile was gone. The man stood straight with his back to the fire.

"Will you come with me to meet with the chief over there, the one in charge of those men in the riot squad?"

"And why should we meet?" Isaac spoke softly but clearly. There were no signs of emotion in his voice. His eyes said more than his words.

"Because," Binet threw caution aside, "damn it, a lot of people are going to get hurt, maybe even killed, and just because the wrong people are confronting each other. Two groups of people are facing each other, not knowing anything of each other, having no respect whatsoever for each other. To me, that makes no sense at all. I'm sure that you have more respect for a moose when you shoot it than you have when you're speaking to me."

The man stared at the ground. With his left hand covering his mouth, he slowly massed his cheeks with thumb and fingers; the man was alone with his thoughts.

"What do you think?" he said, finally.

The young corporal did not take the time to think. His response was immediate.

"Come with me, Isaac. Speak to this man. Tell him of the needs of your people, who you have to speak to in government, who's responsible for all this. Show him, Isaac. Show him the plight of you and your people."

"He's right, Isaac," a voice came from behind. It was the woman Binet had seen earlier at the fire. She approached and stood close to the man.

"This is my sister, Fawn," the man said. He put his arms around her shoulders and the woman moved in closer.

"Yes, we've met," Binet replied.

"Ok, ah..." the man looked at Binet.

"Antoine," the woman looked up at her brother. "His name is Antoine."

"Ok, Antoine," Isaac smiled. "I'll go with you. I'll speak to the man. Then we'll see. Remember what I told you. I'm only a guide to the people."

As the two men crossed the highway Binet saw the chief glancing at his wristwatch. He was convinced that he had gone beyond the allotted time, the five minutes the chief had allowed him.

"Sir," Binet began. "I would like you to meet Isaac, a representative of the people here."

The two men shook hands briefly. Isaac stood calmly with his back straight and his hair waving in the sudden wind that blew across the highway from the west. The chief, with a wave of his hand, invited Isaac to follow him. The two men walked to a section of the highway that seemed, strangely enough, to be void of people, to be set up purposely, it would seem, for the meeting of these two men. There, isolated from the gathering of people, the two men spoke; quietly, seriously, shifting from one leg to another, standing with arms crossed, sometimes with hands held out openly, beseechingly.

Binet could not hear the conversation. No one could hear the words, nor even see their faces the way the two men stood. All they could depend on was the stature of the two men and how they held their hands out. So far, Binet believed, things were going well. There was another reason why Binet was feeling self-assured. The woman, Fawn, had remembered his name. She had even supported him. It was thanks to her that this meeting was taking place. Later, when all this was over, he would try to meet with her. Binet looked towards the kitchen tent across the highway. Someone had added wood to the fire and the flames waved wildly in the wind. As his gaze returned to the pavement, Binet saw his duty belt lying there with its revolver and other items. He wondered, briefly, if he would ever wear that belt again.

The two men, Isaac and the chief, returned to the line-up. The chief spoke to his men. They had stopped the beating of their shields during the meeting. Now, they lowered their batons and shields but remained standing at attention. The chief turned to Isaac and the two men shook hands warmly. Isaac then leaned closer and spoke into the chief's ear. The chief laughed suddenly and handed the megaphone to Isaac.

Isaac held the megaphone up at face level and spoke into the microphone. Only Isaac and his people could understand the words. There was a sudden cheer from the men along the banks and from the women lying on the pavement. The children were not sure why, but they joined in the cheering and clapping. When the cheering subsided, Isaac looked back at the chief and his men and lifted the megaphone up once again and spoke into the microphone.

"I would like to express my thanks," Isaac began. "In the name of my people, I wish to say thank you for the understanding we have found here this afternoon. This day could have ended very differently. A short while ago, standing by the side of a road, two cultures offered respect to each other. This gesture has brought about peace between us. And now, I would like to show you the faith we have in this newfound peace, and the talks we will share with your government people in the future."

Isaac returned the megaphone to the chief. The two men looked at each other and Isaac winked at the chief as he turned to leave. Isaac walked to the middle of the road where he stood surrounded by the women and children. He smiled and raised his right arm and closed fist up above his head. There was a sudden movement of branches behind the men with the placards. Then men came out of the bush, walking slowly but deliberately, down into the ditch and up along the pavement. There were fifty men on both sides of the pavement, maybe more. Each man held a 30-30 Winchester repeating rifle aimed towards the ground.

The squad glanced at their chief; they were set for the attack, guns or no guns. But the chief was not looking at them. Isaac and the chief stared into each other's eyes, both men waiting for what they knew would happen next. As Isaac slowly lowered his fist, the men with the rifles dropped their weapons gently upon the pavement.

Oakie and Kimo

-1-

From the bow of the freighter sled to the tip of the leader's nose was forty feet, forty feet of muscled, longhaired Malamutes in leather harnesses, pulling with their heads down and ploughing through the deeply-packed snow. It was a long way around to the camp but at least the trail was flat on the lake and there were no windfalls to deal with. The last storm had felled many balsam and spruce trees across the trail through the bush and the trees that came crashing down did not always lie flat on the ground. Kimo had shafts attached to his harness but regardless of how long they were or how high Kimo could jump, he could never lift the sled up and over those fallen trees. Kimo was a good dog. He had a heart as large as his head if one could judge its size by the effort he put into his work. Besides fighting and eating, pulling the freighter sled was all he lived for, that, and Oakie, the Siberian-Malamute bitch. Oakie was the lead dog on the team. She was the mother of the six other Malamutes, all sired by Kimo. The eight Malamutes were an excellent team of sled dogs. They pulled together well and fought only when there was nothing else to do.

Tom Franklin was a guide of sorts. He took tourists into the bush for a week of winter camping and travelling with a sled-dog team. But Tom wasn't really a guide. He was just a man who loved to be in the bush with his team, working the trails and spending his nights in a canvas tent with a little tin stove and the smell of balsam boughs rising from beneath his sleeping bag. Still, the tourist trade put gas in his old pickup truck, oil in the Aladdin lamp in his cabin, and food on the table. The money was good; one run with six tourists for six days would keep his Malamutes in food for a whole year. And besides, Tom enjoyed the Europeans, the way they spoke, and their fresh attitude to the forests that he led them through.

On this particular day in February, Tom was headed to his camp just in off Mishigamà Lake. The lake had been named Mishigamà, which, in the language of the Anishinàbek, describes it as a big lake. And it was a big lake with a set of rapids at its northern extremity and an island roughly halfway along its seven-mile length. Tom loved the Mishigamà in winter for its flat, snowy highways. In summer, he paddled its waters as often as he could manage, taking advantage of the many portages from its shores to other smaller lakes.

It was a cold, grey day. In the upper sky, a sundog predicted another storm. Part way along the trail, a northwest wind picked up and forced him to raise his parka hood. He checked the thermometer hanging from the backrest of the sled: minus thirty degrees. The dogs were working well. In another half hour they would be there. He had left his home cabin some time around noon. At the rate they were travelling, they should reach camp by four that afternoon.

When they reached the south shore landing of the Mishigamà, the trail was clearly visible, much more so than on the lake. Thick spruce and balsam trees and tall white pine protected the trail from blowing snow. The trail was firm and he could feel the sled moving faster as the dogs' feet gripped the wind-hardened snow. Less than ten minutes after leaving the lake, Tom called out softly to the team. "Haw Oakie," he said. "Good girl. Haw now." The Siberian-Malamute bitch lunged to the left, onto a narrow snowshoe trail, with seven dogs pulling behind her.

Tom stepped off the runners to allow the sled to turn more easily. Once on the snowshoe trail, he hopped back onto the runners. "Okay guys! Let's go now," he shouted. The pace increased immediately and soon all eight dogs were loping along the trail and down a long winding slope. At the end of the slope, there was a bridge that crossed the stream from Picotte Lake. Just before the bridge a trail veered to the left and went on a hundred yards to Tom's winter camp.

Tom stepped lightly on the brake going down the hill. He slid off the runners near the bridge, running behind the sled as the team headed left to the camp. "Good boys!" he called after them. "Good girl, Oakie!" The eight dogs ploughed through the snow with their tails held high and smiling their dog smiles. They were home. And that was exactly how Tom felt upon arriving at the site, seeing the round, canvas tent with its snow-covered fly and the tiny metal stovepipe sticking out the front. It was the feeling of finally coming home, of being where you belong.

"Whoa," Tom dragged out the word. It was more a statement than a command to stop. They had arrived. The eight Malamutes lay in the snow, panting rhythmically, puffs of steam rising from their extended tongues. But they were not tired. They were in good shape and they loved to run, to hike out to camp on such a cold winter day.

Tom walked through the knee-deep snow to the front of the tent. He struck the tent fly with the handle of his axe and immediately snow began to flow downward, like an avalanche, building up around the wall of the tent. It wasn't long before the fly was completely free of snow and waving in the wind. It was a solid canvas tent, dating back to the Second World War, its age and origin indicated in black on the brown canvas, just above the door, *Ottawa-1944*. It was a circular tent, eighteen feet in diameter and seven feet tall at the centre pole. What was really nice were the four-foot walls that allowed anyone sitting there to lean back and rest their heads against the wall without having to lean forward like in most of the prospector tents he used on the trail. The sweet smell of balsam fir greeted Tom as he opened the door. The bed with its twelve inches of feathered balsam boughs took up half the floor space. Every fall, fresh boughs were added to the previous year's bed and this accounted for its thickness. In front of the bed was the little tin stove, its three-inch-diameter pipe rising and turning sharply and, finally, going out through the canvas just below where the roof ended.

Tom noted the box full of kindling, finely split dry cedar that had been cut and gathered by his last group of tourists. Jean-Marc had spotted the dead cedar along the creek from Picotte Lake. After cutting down the tree he had dragged it back to camp, sawed it into stove wood lengths, and then split some of it into kindling. His wife, Karine, carried the kindling inside and filled the box. She had collected birch bark earlier and placed it next to the kindling, all within easy reach of the stove.

The stove door creaked on its rusty hinges as Tom opened it. He placed two pieces of split ash inside and added a handful of birch bark between them. He covered the bark with kindling. Striking the wooden match against the stove door, Tom placed its flame beneath the bark. Instantly, the bark crackled and spewed black fumes along with its orange-yellow flames as they licked the dry cedar kindling.

After a few moments, Tom added two more pieces of split ash; dead, dry ash they had found in the swamp below the bridge. He closed the door, leaving the draft holes open. He checked the damper on the stovepipe to make sure it was open there as well and then went outside. Smoke billowed out from the stovepipe, carried away in clouds by the wind. He left the tent door open. The roaring fire inside would chase all the cold air out. Later, he would close the door and it would grow warm and comfortable inside.

Now that the fire was going he could go about his other chores. It was important to do first things first, and no others. Tom turned back the tarpaulin and, lifting out a small canvas bag from the sled, he smiled; one of his tourists had written "Parking" on the bag with a black felt pen. Tom removed the stake line from the bag and extended the chain to its full length, anchoring it to sturdy spruce trees with a nylon rope at both ends. After removing a dog's harness, Tom walked it to its place on the stake line and secured it for the night. Each dog would look at him expectantly, waiting for the habitual hug and praise. No matter how the dog had behaved on the trail that day, Tom could always find kind words and a warm hug for his furry friend. The last dog taken out of harness was Oakie. She occupied a special place on the line, next to Kimo.

When all of the dogs had been cared for, Tom began to transfer supplies from the sled to the tent, placing each item in its allotted spot. The naphtha lamp and fuel he set down by the door. Inside the tent and onto the bed of branches, he tossed in his sleeping bag, canvas bags of food, kitchen utensils, and finally, his backpack containing all of his other gear. The last bag to be brought inside was the sled pack that was always tied to the backrest of the sled. In this pack were all the maps of the area he travelled, along with compass, matches, a thermos bottle for tea, a first-aid kit, and a repair kit for the harnesses and the sled. To some it seemed like an enormous amount of equipment but Tom had been doing this for a long time. And always, he kept cutting back, trying to keep things simple while at the same time ensuring that the trips were safe and the nights as comfortable as they could be. It was important to feel good, to be well rested for the next day on the trail. Tom removed the canvas tarpaulin from the sled and took it inside the tent. There, he placed it over the balsam boughs. He checked the fire, added more wood, and closed the tent door. The cold air had finally left the tent and, already, it was beginning to warm up inside.

The dogs were always fed first. But he would need water for supper and this task must be done by daylight. He could easily feed the dogs in the dark. Tom grabbed his axe and a large aluminum pot along with the plastic cup from his thermos bottle and went outside. He walked through deep snow to an alder branch that stuck up out of the snow with a pink ribbon attached and waved in the wind. When he reached the alder, Tom brushed the snow away with his hand until he could see ice. The snow was a good insulator and the water had not frozen much since his last visit. Tom knelt by the hole and scooped up water and debris with the plastic cup until only clear water could be seen. Then, with cup after cup, he filled the aluminum pot. Before heading back to the tent, he filled the cup one more time and took a long drink of the clear, cold water.

Tom transferred some of the water to a smaller pot and placed it on the stove. He had enough water for supper and for breakfast in the morning and for cleaning up after. He went outside and overturned the sled, its runners facing skyward. In the morning he would have to scrape the metal-shod runners of frost and ice. He picked up the harnesses and stored them between the runners.

The dogs began to stir. They knew what was coming. As Tom approached the stake line with the dogs' food, they began to whine and howl and pull against their chains. After each dog had received its share of food, Tom stood there awhile, speaking softly to them, telling them what great dogs they were.

When he had finished with the dogs, Tom returned to the tent. He felt the warmth immediately upon opening the door. By this time it was dark outside. There had been enough light for feeding the dogs but he needed more light for working the naphtha lamp. He reached into the backpack for his headlamp and went outside again. He removed the naphtha lamp from its case and, after turning the pump valve to "open," he began pumping air into the lamp. He lit a match and placed it through the hole and next to the mantle. With the regulator open, he listened for the sound of gas entering. Suddenly, a flame appeared, pulsating at first, then steady and bright. He brought the lamp inside and hung it from a peg on the centre pole. The tent took on a whole new look; a cozy, warm, yellow glow filled the circle and the only distraction was the loud, hissing sound that naphtha lamps make.

Tom preferred using candles. But when there were tourists, this was sometimes dangerous. Later in the evening, when he had finished supper and any chores that needed doing, he might read, sitting with his back against his backpack, or do some writing in his journal. Some nights, when he was alone, he would shut down the naphtha lamp early and sit there in the dark, listening to the wood cracking in the little tin stove, and whatever other sounds that arrived from outside. The only light then was what came through the draft holes in the stove door, pulsating light dancing upon the balsam branches scattered about the floor. There were nights when he might hear an owl calling, over and over again, or perhaps a wolf howling. The wolf call would immediately awaken the gang on the stake line. All eight Malamutes would begin to howl in response and they would continue their chant for a minute or more. Then, suddenly and simultaneously, all would stop. Silence again. Only the puffing of the stove disrupted the quiet, or maybe the jingle of a chain outside, then, silence.

Tom checked the water on the stove. He poured some into a saucepan to which he added noodles and dried vegetables; the rest of the water he kept for tea. As the potage simmered on the stove, he took out cheese and bannock left over from breakfast back at the home cabin. There were biscuits wrapped in wax paper and a small jar of pudding for desert. He had all the utensils he needed, one extra large metal cup, and a tablespoon. Naomi used to tease him about that; these were the only utensils he carried because he so disliked washing dishes. She was probably right about that, just like she was right about everything else. Well, almost everything.

When he had finished eating, Tom rinsed out the pot and his cup and spoon. He leaned against the backpack and listened to the quiet. When there were tourists this would always be a time of calm conversation, comments on the day, the sharing of emotions. But, alone as he was on this night, Tom sat quietly, enjoying the moment and realizing his good fortune. He thought of how well the dogs had behaved, how the storm had held off and allowed him to make it to camp so early in the day. He listened to the wood crackling in the stove and felt its heat against his skin. The fresh smell of balsam was a reminder of the soft bed beneath him. He was most fortunate indeed. What more could a man want? There was one other want but he tried not to think of her. Naomi lived in town, in another world almost, and he knew that thinking about her now would serve no purpose. Still, he missed her. He knew that her being there would have made a difference. This was what he believed. But his love of freedom, the life he was living, would not allow him to confirm this belief.

It had all started with a casual conversation at a bar in town. Tom had built up a repertoire over the years. There were some girls who loved it while others rejected it with obvious distain. Tom was only thirty, not exactly dead yet. And Naomi was a beauty. Her long black hair glistened in the dull light of the bar, as did her soft, brown skin. It was no more than three or four drinks before it was settled; Naomi would visit him at his cabin the next day. And, sure enough, the next morning Naomi arrived, driving her mother's car and wearing a parka and snow boots. She came bearing home-cooked food from her mother's kitchen. Even more frightening to Tom was that, upon emptying the contents of her backpack, she appeared to have come for a week.

After a short run with the team, they returned to the cabin where Naomi prepared supper and talked incessantly about the dogs: how she loved the pups, and the way Kimo kept things straight with the shafts, and how beautiful Oakie was. Tom lit a candle and dropped a large yellow birch log into the stove. By suppertime it was warm and cozy in the cabin. Supper was followed by quiet talk sitting next to the box stove and then, only the crackling sounds of wood burning and the soft, swishing sounds of them touching and caressing disrupted the quiet. Later, they made love beneath the thick down quilt. When they had finished, Tom left the bed to add wood to the fire. Naomi showed no signs of wanting to leave. Tom asked her if her mother might not be worried. Naomi answered simply that she was twenty-four years old.

The next morning, Naomi prepared breakfast after Tom got a good fire going. She did the dishes and suggested a few changes that might be made to his kitchen. Sometime around noon, Naomi kissed him tenderly, thanked him for the wonderful visit and told him how she was looking forward to the next one, and left.

There were similar visits after the first, but these visits lasted longer, two days, three days, sometimes a whole week. It seemed, as of late, the only time Naomi was not there was when he had a group of tourists to deal with. Then, three months after their first night together, it happened, as casually as it had begun. Naomi began leaving things in the cabin: a comb, a change of clothes, some of her favourite books. The weeklong stays grew longer. Their lovemaking was as passionate as ever but now there were questions attached. Did he love her? Could she stop visiting and simply become a regular part of his life? That was when the whole thing ended; his cabin was too small, he had nothing to offer her, no future, no stability, nothing. Naomi left in tears with all of her belongings in a canvas pack and he had not seen or heard from her since.

Tom regretted thinking about her. Loneliness had crept upon him just because he was going over the details. He shook his head as if to rid himself of the whole ordeal and went outside to gaze at the stars and to relieve himself. Having to crawl out of a sleeping bag in the middle of the night with the temperature hovering around minus forty is never pleasant. He knew some bush men who had to get up during the night. They were older. There were even some who would pee into a bottle while lying inside their sleeping bag. So far, Tom was lucky. After his evening stroll outside, he could hold off until morning.

-2-

It was dark in the tent when Tom awoke. He lit his headlamp and checked the time: six-thirty. It had been a good, quiet night. There was some growling on the stake line and, once during the night, he heard wolves howling off in the distance, and poplars cracking with the cold. He was well rested and eager to begin his day. The fire was out, of course.

He had a thick down-filled sleeping bag that, once zipped up, kept his body warmth inside. But zippered up like that was almost like being a mummy. It took some time to lower the zipper and crawl out of the bag. If ever the tent caught fire he would never be able to get that zipper down in time, another reason for the knife beside his head at night.

Tom, still in his long johns, slipped on a pair of camp moccasins and his parka. He quickly got a fire going in the little stove and stepped outside. He relieved himself and, as he did so, he looked towards the mountain to the East, backlit by the rising sun somewhere behind it. Tom stepped briskly towards the overturned sled. He checked the thermometer: minus forty. As he headed back to the tent, one of the dogs yawned in the dawn light.

Tom added more wood to the fire. He lit a candle and placed it by the stove. It would be daylight soon and the light from the candle was more than enough for making breakfast. Besides, he didn't want to be fooling around with a naphtha lamp at minus forty. He had left the large pot of water on the stove overnight so it wasn't long before the thin crust of ice melted and he could use the water for making bannock. He poured water into a small saucepan to heat up for porridge and hot chocolate and placed the plastic container of peanut butter next to the stove to thaw. With flour and baking powder in a bowl, he added lukewarm water and prepared a bannock, which he fried in a spoonful of bacon grease. Tom added more wood to the fire and leaned back against his pack. Through the slit in the door he could see the sun rising over the mountain peak. The sundog had been wrong. Maybe the storm was meant for later during the day. Tom relaxed and sipped the rest of his hot chocolate. It would be a good day no matter what. He thought about the day and what chores must be done, perhaps none at all. He would just ride. There were so many trails to follow, places where he might snowshoe ahead of the team, swamps to visit and tracks to see, open places where eagles soared in early afternoon.

He began to feel drowsy, what with the heat of the stove and a stomach full of breakfast. The sleeping bag looked tempting. He sat up immediately and began punching the sleeping bag into its sack. Then he rolled the sleeping mat and tied it tight with its nylon straps. There, it was done. The temptation to have an early nap was over. Tom poured water into a small tea pail and placed it on the stove. Shortly after, the water began to boil. He tossed in a tea bag and set the pail down beside the stove. With the water that remained, he washed the few utensils he had used.

His boots sat up against the tent wall, their openings aimed towards the side of the stove. Tom took down the felt liners from the clothesline above the stove and stuffed them into the warm boots. He put on fresh wool socks, donned his jogging pants, a clean sweatshirt and a high collar wool sweater. He slipped on a pair of gaiters, the kind used by cross-country skiers. After these came the thick rubber boots with leather uppers and the warm felt liners. These he laced tightly, going around twice at the tops and making a snug seal with the gaiters. He took the leather mitts down from the line and, inside these, he slid in woollen mittens.

After the dishes were dry, Tom packed everything into their canvas bags. He filled the backpack and placed the thermos of hot tea into the side pocket of the sled pack. He checked to make sure there was a trail lunch in one of the other pockets, a sealed bag of nuts, raisins, dried fruit, and a chunk of semi-sweet chocolate. The trail lunches were prepared back at the home cabin, one for each day on the trail. If it was a really nice day, Tom would sometimes build a fire at noon and make fresh tea.

Tom tossed all of the material to one side, slid the tarpaulin off the balsam bed, and carried it out to the sled. He prepared the sled and harnesses and began loading his supplies. Over the years Tom had learned the importance of a properly packed freighter sled. There was a sense of precision involved—each item in its place—to establish a centre of gravity that would allow for the easy manipulation of a loaded sled. After each item was placed in the sled not an inch of free space remained except for a tiny opening reserved for the stake line which would be loaded last of all.

Tom went back to the tent for a last look, to be certain that nothing had been left behind. There was still plenty of birch bark and the kindling box was three-quarters full. He brought in three armfuls of wood from the stack outside by the door and piled them next to the kindling box. He glanced around him, seeing each part of the whole and, in his mind, offered thanks for his good fortune—sad to leave but happy to have been.

The dogs were excited. They knew it was time. Tom began to harness the team. First Oakie was led to the front of the line and had her harness put on. Kimo was harnessed next, and the two ironwood shafts were attached. Then the other dogs were harnessed each in turn. The eight dogs sat upright, waiting for the call. With most other teams, Tom would have secured the sled to a snow anchor before beginning to harness, or maybe even tied the sled to a tree. But this was a good, well-behaved team and there was no need for such precautions. They would never leave without him. They did once, when the pups were younger. He remembered chasing after them, running out from the cabin in his stocking feet and screaming at them to stop. But that was a long time ago. Now, the Malamutes were a part of his life and he was a part of theirs. There were not many teams like that and Tom realized how fortunate he was to have them.

With the team harnessed and ready to go, Tom packed the stake line and placed it next to the tin stove. Over these he packed a two-man prospector tent, covering all of the gear with the tarpaulin. The last items on the sled were his snowshoes. The load was tied securely with rubber bands fastened to the basket lacing of the sled.

Tom coiled a long white rope attached to a metal ring at the front of the sled. The opposite end of the rope he clipped onto a metal ring sewn into the belt that he wore around his parka. This was in case he should fall off the sled and the team refused to stop. He knew that this wouldn't happen, that they would wait for him if he did fall. Still, it was good to have the rope ready should the team need a helping hand while side crossing a steep slope, or getting out of a hole somewhere. Sometimes he would run behind the sled to keep warm. The rope tugging at his belt kept him going.

When all was done, Tom put on his mitts and stepped onto the runners. "Okay, let's go," he said, softly. There could have been a snowshoe hare running ahead of them the way they scrambled. All eight dogs sprinted forward together, with backs bent and heads down low, loping through the deep snow. It was a good start to a new day.

-3-

On a cold, windless day you can hear your dogs' footsteps as they trot on a packed trail. You can daydream as you stand on the runners, half-listening to footpads on snow and, now and then, trying to match these sounds with the hip movements of the dogs running ahead of you. Of course, if they're loping, you're hanging onto the sled handle and shifting your weight to balance things and keep from falling off the sled.

Tom sang a tune in his head, in time to the footpads of his eight Malamutes up ahead. The sun was just a blur now but the wind had held off. The sky was a dark grey, its clouds laden with snow, but that too had held off. The trail he was on had been travelled earlier by snowmobile. Frank Henri, a trapper he knew, had probably gone by there the day before. The trail had hardened overnight. The dogs trotted along at a good pace, a little over five miles per hour was Tom's guess, maybe more. What was important was that the dogs go along at a constant speed without any urging on his part. There's nothing worse for a team than constant nagging from the musher behind. Now and then Tom would say, "Good boys," or as he sometimes did, "Good girl Oakie, good boy Idlak," and so on until he had named each dog on the team and, each time he did so, the dog named would turn to look at him.

As they went around a sharp bend in the trail Tom noticed a series of deep depressions in the snow. "Whoa," he said, as the sled came abreast of the tracks. Next to the tracks were animal droppings with steam rising from them. Tom noted the urine, a pale yellow with slight shades of red. Perhaps the animal had been gut shot. Tom removed his snowshoes from the sled. He strapped on the snowshoes and turned to look at the team. All of the dogs had lain down on the trail and they looked at him with questioning eyes. "Stay," Tom said to them. He turned to his lead dog. "Oakie, stay now," he said, caressing her thick fur. He turned then and followed the moose tracks into the bush, mostly balsam and young maple trees. As he walked, Tom thought of what he would do if he came upon the animal. There was really nothing he could do. He didn't even have a rifle to put the poor animal out of its misery. Still, he followed the tracks and kept his gaze forward in case the moose had lain down in the snow. The tracks took him into a gulley and up through wild plum trees with prickly thorns. As he came through the plum trees, he found himself back on the snowmobile trail, and still the moose tracks continued. Tom decided to let it go. The moose was moving well. Perhaps he had been wrong about the urine. He had seen no signs of blood since he left the team. He removed his snowshoes and turned to face back along the trail. Tom tilted his head back and whistled what sounded almost like a whippoorwill. This particular whistle tune he had used while training the Malamute pups. This was one of the first things he had taught Oakie when she was a young pup, shortly after being weaned. He didn't have to wait long. In less than a minute, he could hear them, their rhythmic breathing and their loping footpads on the packed snow. Oakie appeared with her six descendants behind her, and behind them was Kimo keeping control of the sled with the long shafts fastened to his harness. The team came to a stop as they reached him. Tom secured his snowshoes to the sled and they were off. "Good boys," he said. He had run many dogs over the years but this, by far, was the best team he had ever driven and he always wanted to remind them of that.

As always, the team took off with great speed, loping as if chasing game, but they soon settled down to a comfortable trot. That was the nice thing about Alaskan Malamutes; with a loaded sled or an empty one, a well-trained team would travel at a pleasant trot, constantly, and without any urging on the part of the musher. Tom had tried his hand with Siberian Huskies. These dogs, it seemed, were born to run. An older musher once told him that Siberians had body structures best suited for loping while the Malamutes were more of a trotting dog. He compared the two canine species to horses: pure bred racing horses versus heavy harness working horses. Tom preferred the heavily built Alaskan Malamute. Going flat out on a nice clean trail with a team of Siberian Huskies was quite the thrill but he disliked the nervous disposition of the breed. They are a gentle dog and better behaved than Malamutes in terms of dogfights. However, at harnessing time, it was chaos, even a bit crazy at times, each dog jumping and pulling at the traces even before the whole team had been harnessed. Of course, the sled had to be tied down and released only at the last second. There was no question of stopping along the trail and walking away from the team without pressing down a snow anchor or tying the sled to a tree. Failure to do so could mean a long walk home without your team. But they were nice, gentle dogs. During his first years running Alaskan Malamutes, Tom would have to break up fights just about every time he harnessed the team. As he jokingly told his friends, some of the dogs would rather fight than eat. Over time, he was able to weed out the more serious fighters and, eventually, he ended up with two excellent dogs. From these two dogs came the team that pulled his sled on this cold, grey day. Oakie and Kimo were his best dogs throughout several teams and together they had produced this litter of Malamutes, a team like no other he had known.

They were less than a half-hour on the trail, heading southeast, when Tom heard a snowmobile headed in his direction. There were, in fact, two snowmobiles and Tom recognized the drivers immediately. Both men were Wildlife Protection officers, or game wardens, as they were known to local folks.

"*Bonjour,* Tom," Pierre Cadieux said. Both of the men shut down their snowmobile engines.

"*Salut Pierre, salut François,*" Tom greeted the two men.

"No tourists today, Tom?" Pierre inquired.

"No. I'm a free man today." Tom laughed.

"Quiet here, eh?" Pierre looked around him. "You were you at your camp?"

"Yes. I slept there last night."

"That must be nice. I have not done that for a long time. François likes to do that kind of thing."

"You do winter camping, François?" Tom said.

"Yes, sometimes I go cross-country skiing and we use the nylon tents, you know. No stove. Not like you, Tom. Still it is very, how do you say, pleasant. I get much pleasure from this activity."

"*Tom aime tous les plaisirs de la maison*," Pierre teased. "Eh Tom? You like all the pleasures of home in your camp. You got to keep those little French women happy, eh Tom?"

"Not just the women. Me too!" Tom laughed.

"Hey Tom," Pierre was suddenly serious. "You would not have a kind of cotter pin with you? François is ready to lose a ski on his machine."

"Cotter pin?" Tom chuckled. " Let me have a look. I might have something that will do."

Tom opened the sled pack and pulled out a smaller canvas bag, a green army shoulder pack that served as his repair kit on the trail. Inside the bag was an assortment of material and tools for repairing leather harnesses as well as wrenches and pliers, wire cutters and screwdrivers but no cotter pins.

"Sorry, Pierre," Tom said, closing the bag. "But wait a minute. I might have something."

Tom withdrew a white canvas bag from the sled. Inside the bag was the aluminum pot he used for carrying water to the tent. It had a thick wire handle that was just about the right size for a holding pin. Using the wire cutters, he cut off a length from the handle and offered it to François.

"See if this will fit," he said. Tom bent the remaining wire with the pliers, feeding one end through the holder on the side of the pot. The handle was shorter now but he still had a handle.

"Yes," François called from behind the snowmobile. "It fits okay."

Tom handed him the pliers so that he could bend the wire and ensure that it stayed in place.

"I keep telling you guys," Tom said. "You'd be much better off with dogs. They're quieter, and easier to handle."

"And no cotter pins," François laughed.

"That's right," Tom replied. "And you know, I talk to my dogs. You don't talk to those machines, do you?"

"It would be nice working with sled dogs," Pierre said. "But those days, they are over, Tom. Now they want us to be everywhere the same day."

"Anyway," Tom said, "Let's hope that holds up. I'll have to remember to carry cotter pins from now on."

Both game wardens laughed. They started their snowmobiles and, going wide around the team in deep snow, they headed down the trail towards Mishigamà Lake. Tom waved good-bye to the two men and, uttering a soft, whispered call, they were on their way.

The metal-shod runners slid easily on the newly packed trail. The two game wardens had left their truck at the landing where the ploughed road ended and travelled by snowmobile from there. This meant at least another six miles of solid, packed trail. Tom was thankful as he knew that after four of these six miles, he would leave the snowmobile trail and head east up the mountain to Kabeshinàn Lake. That trail was strictly snowshoe packed, if at all. A week ago, Paul Letendre must have gone up to his cabin by the lake as he did every Sunday. On occasion, Tom would accompany Paul on his trek up the mountain on snowshoes. But mostly Tom led the team up another route if the trail was beaten. The trail was longer but often well packed and the hills not so steep. After crossing a beaver dam and making his way over the portage from Makadewà Nasemà, a small beaver pond between two lakes, Tom would head northeast across the Kabeshinàn. The pace would pick up then for the dogs knew the area well: the last little slope of a hill from the shoreline, the low log cabin almost completely covered over in snow, and then their resting place beneath a towering white pine, sheltered from the wind by a thick wall of spruce and balsam.

Tom remembered the snowstorm of several days past and he noted the ever-present grey sky which probably meant more snow still to come. He had not been to Kabeshinàn Lake for more than two weeks. More than likely the trail to Makadewà Nasemà was covered in deep snow. But there was a good chance that Paul had gone up the mountain to his cabin recently, regardless of the weather. Tom decided he would follow Paul's snowshoe trail up the mountain.

Following the game wardens' recently packed snowmobile trail, they suddenly came upon a wide clearing in the forest. The clearing was part of a forestry road in summer. In winter only snowmobiles travelled this road as the snowplough stopped at the landing where the two game wardens had parked their truck. Tom called to the team to turn left, onto the road. They had covered less than a mile when he spotted Paul's snowshoe trail as it left the forestry road and entered the bush. The trail was snow-covered but the depression it made in the surrounding snow was still visible.

"Gee, Oakie," Tom called. The team followed Oakie, turning to the right, leaving the snowmobile track on the road and moving onto the snow-covered remains of Paul Letendre's snowshoe trail. The wind picked up suddenly and blowing snow struck the back of Tom's parka. Once in the bush, there was no wind. It was a pleasant run through jack pine and the tops of blueberry bushes and frozen sweet fern. After this short run, however, things got a little tricky. They had to cross a beaver pond and the ice on both sides of the dam was unpredictable at the best of times. Tom maneuvered the sled along the bunched up branches of the dam as Oakie guided the team along the trail that Paul had trampled. It was a snowshoe trail, not a sled-dog trail; this meant sharp turns and fallen tree trunks to climb over. Were it not for Kimo's enormous strength and the shafts connecting the belly band of his harness to the front sides of the sled, getting up and over these obstacles would mean plenty of pushing and shoving on Tom's part. Once away from the beaver pond, the trail became more reasonable, yet still a two-mile trek up the steeply sloped mountain to Kabeshinàn Lake.

Tom walked behind the sled going up the steep slope. Although the snow on the trail supported his weight, it was still soft and the dogs' footpads slid backwards as they leaned into their harness. The trail itself was fairly straight and there were only three occasions when Oakie and her crew had to jump over a recently fallen tree. Kimo hurdled each of these obstacles. He brought the shafts down upon it, lifting the front of the sled up and over, and pulling it forward over the fallen tree. This was one of his tasks and Kimo never let them down.

As steep as the mountain trail was, it eventually flattened out and led to a clearing with a rocky escarpment to the east. This clearing, spotted with grey, dead trees sticking up out of the snow was the Kabeshinàn Lake beaver pond or, the swamp, as Paul referred to it. Tom was riding the runners now. As they came out onto the frozen pond, he noticed the depression in the snow where Paul had tested the ice and then continued on ahead. That was good enough for Tom. Sometimes the ice was dangerous there, but he trusted Paul's opinion, and Oakie's, of course. She would never lead them over bad ice.

Paul's trail wandered in and around the tall, dead ash trees that stood up out of the pond ice. There were several piles of stove wood stacked along the trail. Sometime around the middle of March, Tom would come by with the team and, making several trips, they would haul the wood up to the cabin. Once there, Paul would help him unload the wood and stack it in the woodshed attached to the north side of the cabin. This would be the year's supply of stove wood until the next spring when they would do it all again. During the summer months, Tom would visit Paul to do a little fishing, either trolling for speckled trout or simply paddling Paul's canoe around the lake. The warm fire and the smell of frying bacon and beans in Paul's cabin always brought back memories of working his team, hauling chunks of dry ash wood up the hill to the cabin and how, every time, Paul would comment on what a well-behaved team of dogs he had. That alone was worth the effort.

Although Tom had travelled this trail numerous times, coming out of the swamp onto the sudden expanse of the lake always produced a sense of wonder and excitement. Tom reached into the sled pack for his binoculars. He scanned the lakeshore, from one side to the other. Paul had told him about the wolf tracks he had seen. He estimated about six wolves, not hunting, simply playing on the lake in front of the cabin. But there were no wolves now. Tom looked at the blowing snow as it swept across the lake and decided he would have to make camp. It would be dark soon. He could try to make it to the Namegos Club cabin, but, since he wanted to hook up with Paul it was better to camp nearby. And besides, Paul would most certainly arrive the next morning. A snowstorm had never prevented him from hiking to "Kabeshinàn," as he referred to his camp at the lake.

"Gee," Tom called. "Gee, Oakie!"

The team moved to the right, into a little bay, a semi-circle in the shoreline, out of the wind and blowing snow.

"Whoa," Tom said, softly.

The dogs lay down in the snow. They seemed to know that this was home for the night. Tom was equally certain of the tasks that faced him before nightfall. He strapped on his snowshoes and stamped out an area of snow on the ice. When he was satisfied with its firmness, he went about cutting poles for the prospector tent and balsam boughs for his bed. There were plenty of dead ash trees in the swamp for both stove wood and kindling and he had gathered a good supply of birch bark on his way up the mountain.

Once the poles were tied and the canvas tent attached, Tom set up the tin stove and its pipes. It wasn't long before he had a good fire going and began moving material inside the tent. When his camp was completely furnished, Tom laid out the stake line and led the dogs to their places for the night. He hurried through the feeding process; it was getting dark and the dogs were growing impatient for their evening meal.

Having fed the team, Tom turned his attention to his own needs. He walked over to a small mound of snow on the ice, just in front of the rock wall and the tall white pine above it. After removing the snow and a thin layer of boughs from the mound, he struck the ice with his axe. Almost immediately, clear water filled the hole. Tom returned to the tent with a pot full of water and set it on the stove. He lit the naphtha lamp and settled into the routine of preparing supper. Outside, the wind picked up again and he could hear it, even above the annoying sound of the naphtha lamp.

-4-

The next morning, Tom Franklin awoke to the sounds of blowing snow. The tent roof waved above him and he could hear the wind whistling through the needles of the pine tree behind his camp. It was after seven. The dogs had been quiet all night. Even now, there was only the wind.

He raised the door zipper and looked outside. The overturned sled was barely visible and the folded leather harnesses nothing more than a mound of snow between the runners. He looked towards the stake line; there was not a single dog in sight. The feeling of panic was immediate. The team was gone! Something or someone had spooked them during the night. Had he failed to tie the stake line properly? Had all eight Malamutes taken off, still attached to their position on the line? Tom knelt before the door, snow striking his hair and face. Then he realized the foolishness of it all. They were a good team. They would never leave him, not even if they were free to run. It was the storm that did it. A snowstorm could play havoc with your mind. The sound of wind and blowing snow was ghostly. The surrounding wall of solid whiteness left one feeling trapped; confined within a never-ending cocoon. Tom stuck his head further out from the tent wall, squinting against the driving snow. He whistled once, and then a second time, the familiar whippoorwill song the dogs knew so well. At the second call, first one dog and then the next pushed its head up through the thick blanket of snow and looked his way. The eight Malamutes seemed annoyed at being awakened for no obvious reason and even Tom felt a bit foolish as he ducked back inside the tent. He returned to his sleeping bag without bothering to make fire. There was only one thing left to do now and that was to sleep until the storm passed.

Tom was awakened suddenly by the sound of barking dogs. He could hear the excitement in their barking; someone or something was approaching the camp. He glanced over the edge of his sleeping bag and saw the zipper on the canvas door moving upward.

"*Kwey!*" a voice called from outside.

Paul Letendre stuck his head in between the flaps of the tent door. His beaver skin hat was covered in snow, as were his eyebrows and his moustache.

"*Et mon vieux,*" he said. "What an hour to be lying in bed."

Tom glanced at his pocket watch. It was eleven thirty, more than four hours since he had awakened the team.

"I was up earlier," he said, almost apologetically. "Storm was pretty bad so I went back to bed."

"It's still bad," Paul said, leaning forward into the tent. He had not removed his snowshoes and he held the flaps of the tent door tightly around him to keep the cold wind from rushing in. "Come up to the shack. I'll have bacon and beans going in no time."

Paul stepped back from the doorway and lowered the zipper, shutting the tent door. Tom could hear the striking of the wood snowshoes as he turned and headed up to the shack.

Tom dressed quickly and began to break camp. He stored all of his gear in the sled and covered it with the tent and, finally, with the sled tarpaulin. He was happy that Paul had made it up to Kabeshinàn, that they would be together for breakfast and a chat in a comfortable warm cabin. Paul was his best friend and mentor and he owed much of his way of life to the man. Although neither Tom nor his friend were Native, their greetings and expressions of gratitude were often Algonquin words they had learned from Anishinàbe friends. Greetings between them was always "*kwey*" and any form of gratitude or thankfulness was expressed simply as "*migwech*."

By the time Tom had finished packing, the dogs were fully awake and pulling at their chains. They followed Tom's every move and barked their impatience. Why were they not being harnessed? Oakie and Kimo sat upright with their shoulders touching and sniffing the air. The odour of Paul's campfire had attracted their attention. The smell of dry pine burning in Paul's barrel stove had reached them despite the strong winds and blowing snow. Finally, convinced that they were going nowhere, the dogs lay down again, curled up in their snow holes, their full tails covering their feet and nose.

Tom strapped on his snowshoes and made his way across the bay, to the rock face along the shore beyond which he knew warmth and food awaited. He looked upwards, beyond the almost vertical wall of granite and quartz and rust-coloured indications of iron, to the white pine that stood before the cabin. He could see smoke rushing by its branches, being speeded along by the wind.

It was a welcome sight. As Tom completed the climb to the cabin, he marvelled at the low, log cabin, almost totally covered in snow, its tiny galvanized stove pipe standing erect in three feet of snow and the grey-white smoke flowing out of it from the fire inside.

Tom entered the screened porch. He laid his snow-shoes on a makeshift table next to Paul's and opened the door. He wasn't sure which reached him first, the heat or the smell of bacon frying in a large pan on the barrel stove. Paul stood leaning on one leg, turning the bacon over with a fork.

"Grab a chair!" he said cheerfully. "It won't be long now."

Paul pried the lid off a plastic container and dropped a chunk of frozen baked beans onto the pan. The beans sizzled in the bacon grease. He moved the bacon strips to one side of the pan and began breaking the beans up with his fork and spreading them around inside the pan.

"Get us a couple of plates," he said. "We're just about ready."

Tom took down two plates from the board shelf and placed them on the table. Also on the shelf and next to the plates was a low-walled wooden box containing spoons, forks, and knives; all three sets of utensils were separated by thin wooden slats. He picked out knives and forks and set them alongside the two plates.

Paul filled the plates with bacon and beans directly from the frying pan. Before sitting down to eat, he placed a metal wash pan on the flat top of the stove and poured water into it from a pail. The only sound in the cabin was the crackling of wood burning in the stove and the scraping of their forks on melamine plates. Paul reached up and removed two cups from nails driven into the edge of the board shelf.

"How about some Kabeshinàn Lake tea?" he said.

"You bet!" Tom replied.

They did not speak during the meal. Tom gulped down the bacon and beans as he always did and Paul spread ketchup over his beans, tossing them around until they were completely covered. But they always ate in silence. No words or comments regarding the meal were spoken; both men knew each other too well for that.

It was almost dark in the cabin. There was only the one window, high above the door, facing south. On a sunny day it allowed plenty of light in, enough even to read by. But this was a stormy day and the lower half of the window was covered in snow. With the fire crackling and the lovely smell of cooked food, the cabin was anything but gloomy. It was just kind of dark inside.

"Say, Paul," Tom began, "did you ever think of opening up the side windows?"

"No."

There were two other windows, one along each wall. They were low-slung windows with their sills at about the level of a chair seat. Both windows had been boarded up with thick planks nailed horizontally from the outside.

"It would make it a little brighter in here," Tom continued, "especially on days like today."

"Well," Paul dragged out the word and took a drink of his tea. "I suppose. That would be okay in the old days. We never locked up a cabin then. We always left a few cans of food and tea, and matches of course. Whenever we left a cabin there would always be a good supply of kindling and birch bark left in front of the stove. And a small stack of split hardwood."

"You still do that now," Tom interrupted. "But now there's a lock on the door."

"Well," Paul's lips were pursed together tightly. With both elbows resting on the table, he held his hands clasped in front of his face. "You never know when some lone traveller might go through the ice, or be cold and hungry on the trail. In the trunk there, you'll find blankets, woollen socks, and an old mackinaw jacket."

Tom had never looked inside the old trunk that sat facing the stove. A canvas canoe hung above one of the bunk beds and two good paddles stood in a corner alongside several bamboo fishing poles, complete with lines, hooks, and lead sinkers. In this simple log cabin, he mused, a person could find just about everything that was needed to survive; the rest could be found in the bush and in the lake. But now, the cabin door was kept locked, a thick rusted chain and a heavy padlock barring entrance inside.

"So what happens now?" Tom asked. "There must still be people going by here."

"Times have changed, Tom," he began. "In the old days I could come here and find a piece of birch bark on the table with words of thanks written on it. There'd be a fresh supply of kindling and birch bark by the stove, and a new stack of split ash. Often the message scribbled on the bark was only one word, *mìgwech*. I knew then that the thank-you note had been left by an Anishinàbe traveller. Most of the people going through here were hunters or trappers."

"I guess there's not much of that any more. Still, someone in trouble would certainly appreciate this warm cabin," Tom argued. "I can't see anyone not appreciating a warm fire and a place to sleep."

"It's different now, Tom. Most people going through the bush now are tourists, sports fishermen, and hunters, not bush people, not an Anishinàbe hunting for food. No one leaves an offering for what they take any more. They just take. They come into your cabin, eat all your food, and burn all your stove wood. Then they leave, maybe taking off with your axe or your canoe. They might even leave the door open."

"So when did you start locking up the cabin? And boarding up the windows?"

"Well," Paul began, "when I started noticing the kind of people that were going through here: no respect for the bush and the animals that live here. That's when I drilled two holes, one in the cabin wall and one in the door. Now I pass a heavy chain through the wall and the door and tie it together with a brass padlock when I leave. Later on, I boarded up the windows. Being so low, a person could easily break in through there."

"Gee," Tom sighed. "I find that kind of sad. It was so perfect before."

"Well, Tom," Paul looked into his empty cup, "you're right there. I find it sad to think that there are some people like that. Not everyone, of course."

As they continued their conversation, Paul began to wash the dishes. Steam rose from the pan as he scrubbed the plates and utensils with a short-handled dish mop.

"Where you headed today?" he asked.

Tom stood up and opened the door. Only the bay was visible, and not much of that. He could not see the sled, or his dogs sleeping in the snow. The Kabeshinàn was a wall of blowing snow.

"Nowhere right now," Tom replied. "Take a look at that."

Paul turned to look out through the open doorway.

"Well," he said, "there are days like that."

Tom smiled. He recalled Paul saying somewhat similar words not so long ago. It had been a bad summer; unexpected chores and personal matters had prevented him from canoeing the Mishigamà or any other lake. He had complained to Paul, how he had not dipped a paddle into water once that summer. Paul's response then was simply, "Well, there are years like that."

"Say," Paul turned to face him. "You got lots to eat, for you and the dogs?"

"Oh yeah," Tom said. "Good for two or three days, maybe four."

"Why don't you spend the night here?" Paul hung the dishcloth from a wire suspended above the stove. "There's lots of wood in the shed and a good bed to sleep on. A bush guy I know hauled all that up here with his dog team."

They both chuckled over that. Yes, it was true. Tom and the team had hauled the wood in during the previous spring, and the bunk beds several winters before that.

"Well, I suppose. The sled's all loaded, ready to go. I could bring the team up here for the night."

"Well yes, and the dogs will be better up here, out of the wind."

There was a galvanized metal pail, half full of water, by the stove. This was water that Paul had carried up from the lake after his visit to the tent that morning. He dipped the saucepan into the pail.

"Good for some tea?" he said, placing the pan on the stove. He opened the stove door and tossed in two chunks of dried pine. "I picked up some dough-nuts at the bake sale yesterday."

"Always good home-cooked stuff there."

"Well, that's true enough. You should go some-times. Some pretty young women there too."

"Yeah, I suppose," Tom replied.

Paul opened the brown paper bag and took out the two doughnuts. He flattened the bag and set the doughnuts on it.

"Help yourself," he said. He reached over for the saucepan on the stove and poured the golden liquid into the cups.

"*Mìgwech*," Tom muttered. He picked up one of the doughnuts. It had a homey smell and he tried to imagine the hands that had made it. Why did that suddenly make him think of Naomi? He didn't know. He had never seen her making doughnuts. "So, Paul, do you know who made the doughnuts?"

"Name on the package said N. Charland."

Nicole Charland. Naomi's mother was forever bringing food to the church bake sales.

"Probably Naomi's mother," Tom said.

"Well," Paul cradled the cup with both hands, "that could be. I see her often at mass on Saturday evening. I haven't seen Naomi for some time though."

And so the conversation went. Tom mentioned how he had not spoken to Naomi in at least three months, since their relationship had come to an end. And Paul reminded Tom that he wasn't getting any younger, that he had better get out there and check other fish in the pond and see to it that his bloodline did not end with his passing.

"Well," Paul said, at last. "Guess it's time."

Tom opened the door. It was growing dark outside. The wind had died down and snow fell in large, slow-moving flakes.

"Storm's over," he said.

"Should be good heading back," Paul said, as he threw things into his canvas packsack. He never left garbage of any kind. Everything went into the pack-sack. He taught Tom this lesson many years before; when you leave the bush it should always look as if no one has ever been there.

"Be good," Paul said as he ducked under the door-frame going out. Paul was a tall man who always walked with his back straight. This doorway was the only place Tom had ever seen him walk with his back rounded. It was strange seeing Paul strap on his snowshoes, preparing to head home. And there he was, on the porch step without even his parka on, saying good-bye and wishing his friend a good trip home.

"See you maybe next week, Paul." Tom said. "I might head into town. And don't worry. I'll lock up before I leave."

"Oh, I'm not worried."

Without another word, Paul turned and headed down the trail to the lake. Tom stood on the porch steps waiting to see him pass by on the lake, just in case he might look up and wave. Paul walked past the escarpment. He glanced at the dogs on the stake line but he did not look up towards the cabin and he did not wave. One moment he was there, his black parka and beaver hat, with his canvas pack limp on his back; and then, there was only his trail and the snow falling upon it.

After a while Paul's presence was gone from the cabin just as the heat left it when Tom neglected to add wood to the fire. It was different. Although Tom was overjoyed by the fact that he would be spending the night there, the cabin was not the same now that Paul had left. He looked at Paul's chair, the dishpan hanging from a nail behind the stove, the little dish mop beside it. These were reminders of his friend but they could not revive his presence in the cabin. It suddenly occurred to Tom just how important a physical presence can be and how little thought is given to this while experiencing the presence itself. Tom felt a sudden sadness come over him.

As he did every Sunday, just before leaving, Paul had split and stacked several chunks of hardwood against the trunk just in front of the stove, along with a few handfuls of kindling and several sheets of birch bark that he withdrew from his stash under one of the bunk beds. Tom tossed two good chunks of hardwood into the stove, reminding himself that he must repeat Paul's gesture before he left the next morning.

Tom put on his parka and went outside. He strapped on his snowshoes and followed Paul's trail down to the lake. The dogs grew excited as he approached the sled. He slipped the snowshoes onto the sled and, shaking the snow from the collars, he laid the harnesses out in a straight line. As he went to each dog on the stake line he saw their snow holes, almost a foot deep, where they had spent all of the night before and part of the day. After each dog had been harnessed and the stake line stored in its canvas bag, Tom called to the team to head out. Oakie walked a wide semi-circle away from the campsite through deep snow and then she picked up Tom's snowshoe trail. Tom called out, "Head Oakie," and the pace quickened. The team followed the fresh trail, off the lake, past the thick cedar trees, and up the slope to the cabin. Tom stepped off the runners going up the hill. As Oakie reached the furthest edge of the porch, she veered to the right. There, beneath the tall white pine and the thick wall of spruce and balsam was their resting place for the night. Tom set up the stake line and the dogs were soon in their night places, waiting for supper to be served. They had not long to wait. After Tom removed the food bag, his lamp, and his sleeping bag from the sled, he fed them, and thanked them for being there.

-5-

After supper that night, Tom read entries in the logbook, some dating back to before he was born. He sat by the stove, reading and trying not to pay any attention to the hissing of the naphtha lamp. Finally, it got the better of him. He lit a candle and shut down the lamp. With the candle on the table behind him and his legs stretched out by the stove, Tom read on and then, he was on his knees in a wood-canvas canoe, paddling the Kabeshinàn with the others, catching great speckled trout and enjoying portages and stories told by the open fires of shore lunches. It was another time, a far away era. Tom loved to read these accounts and see them in his mind. But the heat from the great barrel stove finally got to him. His eyelids grew heavy and he knew it was time. Tom threw a chunk of dry pine into the stove. It wouldn't last long, he knew, but it would create great light rays in the cabin and the sounds of its burning would lull him to sleep. From habit, Tom placed his knife and his headlamp and pocket watch next to his rolled up wool jacket on the bed. With one puff, he extinguished the candle.

Lying there in his sleeping bag, he could see the light rays darting forward through the crack around the stove door. The wood snapped and crackled as he knew it would. Once, he heard a dog growling. Then, silence, total silence. There was light in the cabin. Tom looked up to the window, above the stove, and saw the moon sitting motionless, as still as the branches on the trees, as quiet as the shadows she created inside this low wooden shelter.

When Tom awoke, it was cold in the cabin, freezing cold. He slipped out of his sleeping bag, put on his moccasins, and started a fire. When the fire was going well, he quickly returned to his bed. This was a cabin, not a tent and he knew it would take longer to heat up. Besides, it was still dark out. Tom pulled the bag up around his ears and waited for sleep to come. But sleep would not come. Paul's words haunted him; he had not seen Naomi in a long time but he saw her mother at church every Saturday. Naomi never liked going to church. The only reason she went there on Saturday evenings was to be with him. And the only reason Tom attended the service was to be on her mother's good side. Probably Naomi stopped going to church after their breakup. Perhaps she had moved away. She was forever speaking of leaving her mother's house, trying to lead a life of her own. She would have moved in with Tom but his cabin was too small. At least, that's what he claimed. But both Tom and Naomi knew very well that the size of his cabin had nothing to do with it. Tom's fear was the problem, not the space he lived in. It was his fear of confinement, of commitment, the sudden changes this might bring to the life he loved.

Tom awoke suddenly It was freezing cold in the cabin. But it was not the cold that had stirred him from sleep, nor thoughts of Naomi. There it was again, a growling, snarling sound. It was not a Malamute growl. Of that, he was certain. Tom dressed quickly and went outside, holding the door to keep it from banging against the jamb. He moved slowly towards the overturned sled, and the stake line beyond it. There, next to the sled, he saw the wretched animal and his heart went out to it. It was an adult red fox. Upon seeing the animal, Tom realized immediately what he would have to do. As he watched it, the fox attacked a branch sticking up out of the snow, biting the bark vigorously, and suddenly, diving into the snow and, just as quickly, turning to snarl at Oakie and Kimo who stood only a few feet away. Tom noticed how the animal's fur seemed to be totally drenched, and that saliva was flowing from its mouth, splattering around with each jerking movement of its head.

Tom returned to the cabin for Paul's long-handle splitting axe. He could not afford to miss. To do so could mean death for both him and the dogs. Failure to put down the animal would mean a cruel and horrible death for the fox. Tom approached the animal calmly, stepping behind the fox as it snarled at the dogs. He brought the axe down swiftly upon the back of its head. The fox sank forward in the snow. Tom struck again and waited. He watched the animal closely, looking for breathing movements, or any other signs of life. It was over. The dogs whined and pulled at their chains. The fox was dead but Tom's task had only just begun. The saliva still contained the dreaded virus, as could the kidneys and some of the tissues. He would have to destroy the animal, completely.

Tom had, in years past, witnessed the convulsive phase in animals infected with the rabies virus and he was taking no chances. After exposing the axe head to flames in the stove, he returned to where the fox lay, carrying a long steel poker and a cardboard box he had found in the shed. He maneuvered the fox into the box with the poker, taking care not to touch any part of the animal with his mitts. He then dragged the box over the snow, to a clearing behind the shed where he made a bed of split, dry pine. He placed the box on the split pine and doused the fox in naphtha gas from his fuel can. Next, he covered the fox with short lengths of split ash. After wrapping a strip of birch bark around a balsam sapling, he put a lighted match to the bark and tossed the flaming bundle onto the pile of split ash and the fox beneath it. With a loud "Woosh" the mound was immediately enveloped in flames. The dogs, although at a safe distance, whined and pulled nervously at their chains. Tom returned to the cabin. He slid the end of the poker into the stove and left it there a long while. He would stay longer than planned at the cabin. He must make sure that the fox was thoroughly incinerated. And he must tell Paul about it. In the spring, they would bury anything that was left of the animal. After breakfast, Tom went outside to the fire. There, he offered tobacco for the taking of the animal's life.

Back in the cabin, Tom completed the tasks of washing dishes and replenishing the woodpile in the same manner and order as if it was Paul Letendre himself performing them. Paul was his teacher, his mentor, and Tom took great care in following his teachings as best as he could; the driving force, the reasoning, if any, behind his behaviour was simply that Paul would expect it of him.

Tom wrote an entry in the log, just below Paul's. First, he read Paul's entry: hiked up to camp. Strong winds and blowing snow. Tom Franklin camped at lake near swamp, came up with team of Malamutes. There was no mention of how Tom had slept in until eleven thirty and how Paul had fed him breakfast and offered him a place for the night. That was Paul. Tom completed his entry, including a detailed account of the rabid fox. After one last look around the cabin to make sure that all was as it should be, he fed the chain through the hole in the door, snapped the padlock in place and left. He went directly to the loaded sled and the eight Malamutes lying in the snow, harnessed, and looking forward to being on the trail again.

Going by the wood shed and down the hill to the lake, Tom held his foot on the brake. After their prolonged rest period the day before, the dogs had plenty of energy to burn and the steep, narrow trail down to the lake was not the ideal environment for a sudden surge of pent-up energy. As the team approached the entrance to the swamp, near where they had spent the previous day, a decision was called for. Would they follow Paul's snowshoe trail across the swamp ice and down the two-mile slope to the beaver pond, or should they chance going south along the Kabeshinàn shoreline to the Makadewà Nasemà and down the alternate trail to the forestry road. There was no visible trail on the lake. The previous day's storm had erased all signs of earlier trails. Tom stepped off the runners to test the snow. It was as he suspected: he would have to snowshoe in front of the team, at least while crossing the lake.

It was a beautiful, sun-shiny day, no wind to speak of, and, despite the fox incident, they were enjoying an early start. Tom pulled the snowshoes from the sled and harnessed up. He walked to the head of the team and began the slow rhythmic snowshoe hike across the Kabeshinàn. The snowshoes sank about six inches but the new snow was light and fluffy which made walking easy. What helped even more was that Tom remembered how his trail from previous trips followed the shoreline and this provided him with a firm, packed surface beneath the six inches of loose snow. Once in the bush, he thought, the trail would be hard enough to allow him to ride the sled..

It was exactly as he had imagined. As they left the lake and approached the portage, the trail was clear. There was some snow but not enough to warrant wearing snowshoes, so he removed his snowshoes and ran behind the sled as the team moved up the portage trail and on to the Makadewà Nasemà. There the wind had covered the beaver dam in a thick blanket of snow. Tom walked ahead of Oakie, feeling along the edge of the dam with his feet. The snow was up over his knees in places. Oakie followed close behind him and Kimo, straining against the shafts, kept the sled from sliding off the dam.

Up ahead, Tom could see the trail again, and the thick cedar bush on both sides. Finally, they made it across the dam and onto the trail only to find another surprise awaiting them. As the team came out from the Makadewà Nasemà, a fresh snowmobile trail ran directly in front of the team and disappeared in a maze of frozen alders. Tom smiled, almost certain who had gone by there. After examining the tracks more closely, he could not be sure about the time but he was certain that whoever had gone by there had not come out, at least not on this trail. It was Tom's guess that Frank Henri had gone in earlier that morning to check his traps at Asin Lake. That alone was enough for Tom. He would head in to Asin and try meeting up with Frank. The dogs waited, panting easily, their thick red tongues exposed to the cold air. "Haw Oakie," Tom said, softly, and the team moved silently to the left, following the freshly packed trail.

Travelling was easy on the packed trail. Within minutes they descended the steep bank to Asin Lake. And Tom had guessed right: less than a hundred yards from the portage and next to the escarpment along the shoreline he spotted the yellow snowmobile. As they came alongside the machine, Frank waved to Tom and the team from a clump of spruce saplings. He held a small belt axe in his hand.

"Any luck?" Tom called out as he stepped off the runners. All eight Malamutes stared at the trapper.

Slowly, one after another, the dogs settled down in the snow but their gaze remained fixed on the bearded man coming out of the bush.

"No, not today," Frank replied. "It was better down by Picotte. I got some nice martin there, day before yesterday."

"I saw your tracks." Tom said. "Later, I met up with Pierre Cadieux and François. They were headed in to Mishigamà. Did you sleep over at your shack last night?"

"No. Storm was pretty bad. I came in early this morning."

Frank had a small cabin along Madàbì Lake about a two-mile straight-line distance from Kabeshinàn. It was a square timber cabin, built sometime in the late thirties and Frank had acquired it from the Lands and Forests people in town. There were names and dates carved into the logs, names of people that were long gone which added a sense of history to the cabin. Tom had discovered Paul's name on the outside of a bottom timber, his name and the year 1941. Paul told him that he remembered being there, just before he left to go overseas to war.

"I was camped at Kabeshinàn night before last," Tom explained. "Slept in Paul's cabin last night. I sure was glad to meet up with Paul."

"Guess he's still there, then?"

"Oh no. He left yesterday around five."

"Are you sure about that?" Frank looked suddenly very serious.

"Yeah. Storm was over then. He headed down by the swamp."

Frank packed his axe and a small packsack into a wooden chest attached to the rear of his snow-mobile.

"Listen, Tom," he said, "I don't want to worry you but Paul's truck was still at the landing when I came in this morning. Maybe it wouldn't start yesterday."

The landing was a clearing at the end of the main road. It was the remains of an abandoned effort at farming made more than fifty years earlier. The landing, as it became known, was the end of the line for all motor vehicles during the winter months. In summer, there was the forestry road but during those times when snowfall reached up to your knees, people left their trucks at the landing and went on to the bush by snowmobile, or dog team, or on snow-shoes as Paul always did. The landing was where the two game wardens had parked their truck before heading out to Mishigimà Lake.

"That could be," Tom replied. He was worried. Paul took good care of his pickup truck. "Were there any tracks around the truck?"

"I didn't check. With the storm and all, I just fig-ured he spent the night at Kabesinàn."

Tom felt sick. He tried to chase the thoughts out of his mind but they kept coming back, loud and clear, the swamp, the beaver pond, the tall, grey *chicots*, and the bad ice.

"I'm going back, Frank," he said.

Tom walked up to the sled and called out, "Oakie! Come 'round, Oakie!"

The dogs were on their feet in an instant and, as Oakie ploughed a wide semi-circle through the deep snow, Kimo leaned into his harness and turned the sled around while the other six Malamutes pulled vigorously in their traces.

"Hang on, Tom!" Frank shouted behind him. "I'll go ahead as far as the swamp."

Frank pulled the starter cord and the engine roared after the second pull. He swung a leg over the seat and headed off across the lake and up the portage trail with Tom and the team following behind. It wasn't long before he lost sight of Frank but he could hear the whine of the snowmobile engine as it sped along the trail through Makadewà Nasemà and on to the Kabeshinàn. Tom ran behind the team, yelling, "Head Oakie! Head!"

The team trotted at a brisk pace, then loped on the flat parts of the trail. Tom ran and pushed and urged them on, stepping onto the runners only when they were loping well. They could sense the urgency in his voice, it seemed; he had witnessed this reaction once before, on the Tendesì, a small, bird-shaped lake northeast of the Mishigamà. That day, after going over the portage from the Mishigamà, Tom headed across the Tendesì but did not bother to check the ice as the thermometer had gone down to well below minus forty the night before. Half way across the lake, he felt the runners suddenly drop and water rise close to his knees. "Head Oakie! Head Kimo!" he screamed. The dogs had been trotting along at a good pace but upon hearing his cry they broke into a lope, Kimo's hind legs touching water as the ice crumbled before the sled. But they made it. The team had managed to haul the sled to stronger ice and Tom was forever grateful for their efforts. He was convinced that they had understood the panic in his voice. They had reacted to his plea and, now, racing down the Kabeshinàn, they were responding to his cry for help once again.

Tom ran as best he could, hopping onto the runners only when he felt winded. He could see the entrance to the swamp but there was no sign of Frank or his snowmobile. As he arrived at the entrance to the swamp, he could hear the snowmobile engine. Soon after, Frank appeared, standing upright on the running boards. He waved to Tom, a back-and-forth wave that Tom understood to mean, no sign of Paul. There was that at least: he had not gone down beneath the swamp ice.

"Went right to the end of the swamp," Frank explained above the clatter of the engine. "I could still see his tracks going out."

"*Mìgwech* for that," Tom said. He leaned on the handle of the freighter sled. The dogs panted heavily and stared at Frank as they had done earlier. They never seemed to smile at the trapper. Perhaps it was his full beard. Or the thick wolf fur cap he wore. "At least we know he made it through the swamp."

"All that's left is the pond below. Don't think I could make it down with this thing." Frank pointed with his thumb to the snowmobile with its motor idling roughly, the extra long track, and the two skis protruding out the front. "Think you can go down with the team?"

"Sure," Tom replied. "It'll be standing on the brake most of the way. I've done it before."

"I'll go back along the lake and down the other way." Frank straddled the narrow seat and prepared to leave. "I'll meet you at the beaver dam."

"Okay," Tom replied. He knew that this was the best plan. That way they could cover every possibility. He stepped onto the runners and instantly, all eight Malamutes were on their feet. "Head Oakie! Hike!"

The team loped through the swamp as they never had before. Tom pushed with one foot, trying desperately to follow the rhythm of his dogs. But he could not run fast enough to be off the runners. As they snaked in and out between the grey, dead *chicots*, Tom grasped the centre of the sled handle to keep his hands from being smashed against one of the dead trees. Once out of the swamp, it would be different. There, it would be downhill all the way, with sharp corners and the occasional windfall across the trail. That would be Kimo's time to perform, to lean back in the harness and help Tom keep the sled from running over the team. The brake helped some but the trail was mostly loose snow. It was up to Kimo and Tom knew that the hundred-pound plus Malamute could do it. He had faith in Oakie and Kimo and their six descendants.

"Easy Kimo," Tom repeated over and over again. It was a steep slope, a snowshoe trail, and the several hundred pounds of supplies and musher pushing against the team was no minor detail. Tom stood on the break but the forged metal teeth flowed easily through the loose snow. The snow was too deep for the brake to touch ground. Occasionally, it caught on a branch, or a small tree that lay across the trail. The team walked now but they were still pulling. They were trained to do that. It was up to Kimo to hold back with his strong thighs, and he did his job well, just as Tom knew he would.

As they reached a thick line of alders, Tom realized that they were approaching the next danger zone, the dreaded ice along the edge of the beaver dam. The ice was never good there. Tom knew that and so did Paul. It was getting dark when he left the cabin. It would have been dark when he reached the dam. He might have stepped to the side, or slipped off the dam. Kimo maneuvered the sled around the last tight corner and the beaver dam came into view. Frank was standing on the dam, smoking a cigarette. He did not smile or wave as he had done earlier at the entrance to the swamp.

"Whoa," Tom called, softly. Oakie stood on the curve of the dam, staring at the man who had wolf fur covering his head and part of his face, and smoke coming out of his mouth. If Tom had not been so worried, he might have appreciated the humour.

"So? Any sign?"

"No. Nothing," Frank replied. "We've covered everything. The thing to do now is to go back to the landing. And check both sides of the trail."

"But you came through this morning."

"That's right. But I wasn't looking for Paul. And flat out, this machine really flies."

Tom was relieved and worried at the same time. They had covered the dangerous places. And there was no sign of Paul. The night before, the snow had stopped. It was a clear night. He remembered the moon in the window. The temperature had dropped. He recalled how cold it had been in the cabin. Paul could have frozen.

"You go ahead, Frank," Tom stood next to Kimo. He patted the dog's head as he spoke. "We'll catch up later. You check on the left side. I'll do the right."

Frank walked back to the snowmobile. He had left it on the bank, above the beaver dam. As the sound of the engine faded, Tom and the team made their way across the dam. As they sped through the jack pine and the tops of blueberry bushes along the trail, Tom was troubled. The last thing he wanted to discover was Paul's frozen body curled up in the snow. If Paul hadn't frozen to death and his truck was still parked at the landing, then what? Once on the forestry-road trail, the team trotted along at their usual pace while Tom kept his eyes locked onto the right side of the trail. He could see where Frank had hugged the left side with his snowmobile. It was only a couple of miles but somehow this last part of the trail seemed enormously long to Tom. Every depression, every dark object in the snow brought with it anguish and despair. They went by a crumbling log cabin, its roof caved in and its aspen walls slowly rotting as well. It had belonged to a weekend trapper who had long ago returned to living in the city, abandoning a life he had studied religiously in the novels of Jack London. As they went past the cabin, Tom stared straight ahead. He knew that after the next corner was the landing where Frank had seen Paul's pickup truck. And there it was. Tom ran beside the sled, urging the team on. The truck was there with its hood up and another truck facing it, the two front bumpers almost touching. The other truck had its hood raised as well. Both trucks had their engines running. Tom could see the grey clouds of exhaust fumes coming from the rear of the vehicles.

Upon reaching the landing, Tom saw Frank's snowmobile parked alongside Paul's truck. There was no one in the truck even though the engine was running. He looked towards the other truck. There they were, like three birds on a wire. The driver that Tom didn't recognize sat behind the wheel. In the centre and wearing his beaver hat was Paul, and beside him was Frank smoking a cigarette. Tom waved to all three of them. He smiled and waved

again and, in his mind, words formed spontan-
eously. *Migwech*! Tom offered a silent prayer of
thanks, grateful that his friend had not drowned in
the swamp or frozen to death in the snow.

-6-

Paul seemed embarrassed by all the commotion he
had stirred up. He felt sorry about the worry he had
caused them and he repeated several times how
much he appreciated their efforts, and how he would
be forever grateful for their concern. True, he could
really have been in trouble but, as it turned out, he
was just fine. The driver of the other pickup, Charley
Boudrias, was an old friend of Paul's. He handed out
cups of coffee that he poured from a large stainless
steel thermos bottle as Paul told his story. All four
men stood outside, drinking coffee from Styrofoam
cups and leaning against Charley's pickup truck.

"Well," Paul began, seemingly looking at his boots
in shame, "it all started because of the storm. You
remember that blowing snow, Tom? It got so bad I
had to turn my headlights on just in case I met a car
on my way in. When I got to the landing, I parked
the truck as you see it now, facing south with its grill
out of the wind and the driving snow. Well, you
know how I am, anxious to get moving, to be on the
trail and up at Kabeshinà. Anyway, I locked up and
headed out, never thinking about the headlights. I

was up at Kabeshinàn all day, as you know. I got back here sometime around six. Well, you can guess: when I turned the key, nothing happened."

"So where did you go?" Tom was puzzled.

"Well, I didn't want to spend the night in the truck. No blankets or anything. So I locked up and started walking back to town."

"But that's over twenty miles," Tom said. "Did you make it home?"

"Oh yes. And not too late either. Guess I'd walked about five or six miles when I heard a truck coming from behind. It was Pierre and François from the Wildlife Services. They were on their way back from Washkà Lake. Lucky for me. Anyway, they gave me a ride back to town, right to the house. So, this morning I called my good friend Charley here to see if he could give me a boost."

"It must have been cold on the road. Temperature really dropped last night. Lucky for you those guys came along." Tom felt that he was repeating himself. He was so happy to see that his good friend was still alive that he was unable to come up with the words to describe what he felt inside, how his feelings of gratitude had nothing to do with extreme weather, and game wardens, and a warm ride back to town.

"Well," Paul stretched out the word as he always did, "that's what good friends are for, Tom. It could have been you, or Frank. It could have been you boys finding me somewhere on the trail."

They finished their coffee and Charley closed the hoods on both trucks. He and Paul shook hands warmly. Charley left then, backing away from Paul's truck and then heading down the narrow road to town. Frank explained how he wanted to head up to his cabin at Madàbì Lake, to check the snow on the roof. After a brief handshake with both Paul and Tom, he headed away from the landing. They watched him go, disappearing around the corner, past the crumbling trapper's cabin.

"Well Tom," Paul said, "what you got planned for the rest of the day?"

Tom had not really thought of anything but finding his friend. Before meeting up with Frank, he had thought of travelling down the trail to the Forestry Road and maybe going on to Green Lake or maybe even crossing over to Mishìwaki Lake to visit an Anishinàbe friend who was spending the winter there. But it was late now. He should be thinking of finding a campsite. There was always his base camp at Mishigamà. From the landing, he could be there in an hour.

"Head back to Mishigamà probably," Tom replied. This was Monday. Paul rarely went to his camp during the week. Besides, it was a bit late for that. "How about you?"

"Well," Paul sighed, "too late to head up to Kabeshinàn. I'll head home now. Adèle was pretty worried last night. Don't want to upset her again."

"I'll bet. What time did you get home?"

"About eight o'clock."

"Well, at least you made it."

"Oh yes. Say, Tom, what would you say to a good home-cooked meal? Join us for supper tonight."

Tom was unable to speak. He stood there in the snow with his mitts in his hands. It wasn't often that he was invited out for a meal. His mind was still dealing with the search for his friend and the anxiety and fear of not finding him alive. It was as if he had to slow things down in his mind. Thoughts were going by too quickly; he would have to get home, feed his dogs, get a fire going in the cabin. He would have to try starting his old truck; he hadn't done that in over two weeks, two weeks of minus thirty, minus forty degrees. The silence between the two men became unbearable. He had to speak up.

"I don't know, Paul," he began. "Thanks very much for the invite. But you know, if I go by the road, it'll be two hours at least before I get back to my place. Then another hour, at least, feeding the gang, making fire, and all. Not even sure the old truck will start. Probably have to place hot coals under the motor for twenty minutes or so before it'll turn over. Bad enough Adèle had to wait for you last night without making her wait for me tonight."

There, it was done. He had stated it all, as clear as could be without appearing ungrateful for the gift that had been offered him. It was indeed a gift. He had enjoyed sharing a meal with Paul and Adèle on more than one occasion and, always, it had been a real joy. The food, the conversation after by an open fire, were always most enjoyable: a relaxing experience that seemed almost therapeutic. He had always left Paul's home with new goals and a refreshed attitude.

"Listen here," Paul leaned on one leg, squeezing the leather mitts between his hands. "We can load the sled and the dogs into the truck. I'll drive you back to your cabin. Come down to the house after your chores."

He hadn't thought of that. He was trapped in a sense. There was no way out without insulting his friend and he certainly didn't want to do that. He was grateful to Kije Manidò for protecting his friend. To refuse this offer would somehow throw a shadow upon his previous prayer of thanks to the Great Spirit.

"Okay," Tom said. "But you might have to boost the truck."

"That's not a problem. You got rope? We can tie the dogs to either side of the sled."

And so they began. Tom released the shafts from Kimo's harness. He unhitched the leather traces from the whippletree at the front of the sled. Any other team he would have tied to the front of the truck during these maneuvers, but not these dogs. All eight Malamutes lay quietly on the hard packed snow. They lay there, following the motions of both men with interest. After Tom had tied the shafts to the sides of the sled, he and Paul raised the front of the sled onto the lowered tailgate. Then they lifted the rear of the loaded sled and pushed it into the box of the truck. Tom removed Oakie's and then Kimo's harness and lifted them into the truck, placing them side by side as they would be on the stake line. Each dog was the same, lifted into the truck and tied to the side of the sled. Tom picked up the leather harnesses and stored them in the half-cab behind the seat. Paul slammed the tailgate shut and they were ready to leave. It was warm in the truck. Tom looked through the rear window as they left the landing. All eight Malamutes had lain down, some leaning against each other, and all looking as peaceful as they had on the stake line at Kabeshinàn Lake.

It was about ten miles from the landing to Tom's cabin. The road twisted and turned through jack pine forests and farmers' fields and then along a mountainous area where the long branches of white pine reached over the road, just above the height of Paul's truck. Without warning of any kind, not even a rural mailbox, they came to a narrow entrance that led away from the main road, lined on both sides by tall red pine. The dogs sat upright in the truck. They knew that they were home. Paul drove up close to Tom's truck. It was parked in front of the cabin, covered in snow. Tom led each dog out of the truck and over to a thick group of mature white spruce trees. Some of the lower branches extended sixteen feet or more, forming a second roof over the doghouses. Arriving at a doghouse, Tom would reach inside for the end of the chain and snap it onto the dog's collar. This was followed by a hug and words that only dogs would understand. When all of the dogs were settled in, both men lifted the sled out of the truck. Tom pushed the sled to the front of the cabin, stopping by the steps to the narrow porch. He opened the door to the cabin and went inside. All he needed was close at hand, bark, kindling, and split hardwood. Within minutes, flames shot past the damper key and, "womp, womp" sounds came surging out from the cast iron stove. He opened the top of the stove and dropped two more chunks of wood inside, whole trunks of dry maple. He left the door open while he unpacked the sled and carried material into the cabin.

While Tom was busy firing up the stove, Paul raised the hoods of both trucks and connected the heavy wire cables between the batteries. He waited as Tom finished storing the gear, watching him toss the tarpaulin over a log that extended outwards from the porch. Hanging that way on a sunny day, any ice or snow that might have stuck to the tarpaulin would evaporate without wetting the canvas

"Want to give it a try?" Paul said.

"Yeah, right away." Tom realized that Paul had to be going. He appreciated Paul's help but Adèle was not aware of their plans. She expected her husband back in about an hour or so, just the time it would take to get his truck started and head back home.

The seat was cold, and hard. Tom tried not to breathe lest he fog up the windshield. He held the clutch pedal down, even though the gear shifter was in neutral, and began to turn the ignition key. The key was cold, like handling a solid piece of ice. The key resisted, turning slowly, ever so slowly. Tom feared that the key might snap. Suddenly, it slid, all the way, clockwise. There was a drawn out whirring sound, weak and slow-moving but gradually becoming a fast-spinning whine. Then, it happened. A few short coughs and the engine began to turn on its own. "*Migwech*," Tom muttered. The motor coughed and sputtered and finally settled down to a loud, almost constant, roar.

Tom left the truck idling, a blue-grey smoke coming out from beneath the truck where the exhaust pipe was supposed to be. He turned on the heater fan and went outside. Paul had removed the cables and lowered the hoods on both trucks.

"I'll have supper ready in about an hour," he said

Tom watched Paul back away from the cabin and both waved as Paul headed out to the main road and home.

There was still plenty to be done. Tom hurried through his chores, first things first and the others in their proper time, just as he did on the trail. He added more wood through the top lid of the stove and, finally, he closed the cabin door. He went out though the back door, to the meat cache. He picked out the largest of the beaver carcasses; he guessed it to be a good sixty pounds. Laying it flat on the snow, Tom chopped the carcass into eight thick slices. He loaded the meat into two five-gallon pails and headed to the dog yard. The sounds were immediate: wild crying, howling, barking, and as soon as each dog got its chunk of beaver, the ripping and tearing of the aspen-smelling meat. Normally, Tom would stand there and watch them eat, and speak to them. But tonight, he must hurry. It was almost nighttime. Through the branches of the enormous spruce trees behind his cabin he could see the moon, as bright as the previous night at Kabeshinàn, slowly making its way upward and westward, and soon to be casting its silent shadows upon the snow.

Tom hurried. The rumblings of his pickup truck were a constant reminder. He had to get a move on. Luckily, he had thought to leave a kettle full of water on the stove before going out to feed the dogs. Tom hurried through the sponge bath and put on fresh, clean clothes. The Aladdin lamp glowed silently on the counter, next to the mirror as Tom checked his hair a last time. With the lamp shut down, he added a large unsplit chunk of beech wood to the fire and closed the door behind him.

-7-

Tom's old truck was well behaved on the road to town. But, driving into town always overwhelmed him, with the lights and the traffic; he didn't recognize any of the drivers. Anyone he encountered on the trail was always a good friend, or an acquaintance. If he didn't happen to know the person, it wasn't long before he did. Driving down the main boulevard to Paul's home left him feeling lonely and empty inside. Tom followed the shortest route to Paul's house. The light on the veranda was lit, as were the lights in the kitchen and the living room. This was not something that he was accustomed to. He stood at the door with feelings of apprehension. There was no reason. It was just the way he was. Tom knocked twice and went inside.

"*Kwey!*" Paul greeted him. "Come in! Come in! Take off your coat. Come in the kitchen. I'm almost finished."

Tom removed his jacket and hung it from the coat rack by the door; his heavy boots he left on a rubber mat next to Paul's. Going down the hall to the kitchen, he saw Adèle sitting by the window. Her lips moved silently as she concentrated on a crossword puzzle.

"*Salut* Adèle," Tom greeted the woman.

"Enhenh," she answered, smiling. "We almost lost our chum, eh. Imagine, going out in a storm like that."

"Yeah well, I was out there too."

"I know. You're as crazy as he is." She pushed the crossword puzzle aside. "You know, it could have been serious. Just think. If he had gone through the ice, by the time you got there, it would have been too late. You guys and your bush, I don't know what it is that drags you out there."

Paul walked into the living room carrying a tray with three glasses of white wine.

"This should hold us a few more minutes," he said, handing a glass to Adèle and one to Tom.

"Look at him," Adèle laughed, "trying to make up for yesterday."

"Got to keep the little woman happy," Paul chuckled.

Paul sipped his wine and slipped back into the kitchen, leaving Tom to do some explaining on his behalf.

"I'm the same way," Tom began. "I can't explain it. I just feel better there, in the bush I mean."

"Oh, I know," Adèle tilted her glass and the wine quickly disappeared. "A certain young lady told me about you."

Tom glanced at her smiling eyes. Was she teasing him? Had she been speaking to Naomi?

"Actually," Adèle continued, "she's not so young, Madame Charland that is. I met her after church on Saturday. It's not often we get to chat. I just happened to ask her about her daughter, Naomi. We haven't seen her at church lately. That's when she started talking about you, and your dogs, and your precious bush."

Tom felt his face grow warm. Just the mention of her name stirred up feelings inside him. But to hear that her mother was talking about him, his love of the bush and his dogs, left him speechless. Any words he might utter would be useless, entirely without meaning. It was better to say nothing. But then, he felt obliged to respond, if only to show respect for both of these women.

"A very nice woman, Madame Charland," he began. "I haven't seen her in quite some time, not since Naomi and I split up. I don't think that Madame Charland liked me very much. The thing about the bush and the way I live, you know; no future and no steady income. I think that bothered her. It doesn't make a good match for her daughter."

"I don't think so, Tom," Adèle said, softly. "You know, women don't always say the things they mean. Madame Charland, Nicole, thinks quite highly of you. No, no, don't laugh. She does."

Tom drank the rest of his wine. He disliked the subject. It was like walking on bad ice where you have to use a pole and keep striking the ice with it. If you hear a hollow sound you have to back-pedal quickly. If you fail to do so, down you go. And once you go down, you're down.

"And her daughter," Adèle continued, "well you know Naomi. Nicole tells me that the poor girl is not the same. Every time the phone rings, or the postman drops a letter in the mailbox, she rushes to it, hoping it's news from you. She's a very sad and lonely young woman, Nicole told me."

What could he say? He didn't have a phone and he was not in the habit of writing letters. But he did miss her. There was no doubt in his mind about that.

"I'm really sorry for Naomi," he said at last. "It's just that the way I live, I don't think it's for her. She'd be better off with some guy in town here, with a nice house, and a steady job, you know."

"No, I don't know!" Adèle pretended to be angry. "You should have seen the shack that Paul and I started out with. Eh Paul?" She raised her voice so that Paul could hear her in the kitchen.

"Eh, what's that?" Paul said, looking around the kitchen doorway, into the living room.

"I was just telling Tom how it was when we first got together, about the shack we lived in that summer."

"Well," Paul began, "You know how it is. Worked hard all day and at night after supper I'd add a few boards to the walls. The walls were just tarpaper spread over a spruce-pole frame. We were living up at Venn Depot then. Remember Adèle, we used to build a fly-net cage around Marie to keep the black flies away. After a month or so, we had a nice warm shack."

"Those were some of the best years," Adèle added. "Marie was only a baby then. Henri wasn't even born yet. So you see Tom, you can never tell how we women really feel. Did she ever once say to you that she did not like the bush, that she hated it enough not to be with you, eh?"

The woman stared hard at Tom, waiting for some response but none came. Finally, she glanced up at Paul, hoping that he would add support to her words.

Paul held his lips pursed together. Tom expected to hear the usual drawn out, "well" but Paul was silent, staring into the eyes of the woman he loved.

"Supper's ready," he said finally. "You know, Tom, I don't want to get mixed up in this affair. I know how you feel about the bush and the life you lead. I didn't want to mention this but I got a phone call from Naomi last week. I spoke to Adèle about it, but no one else. Adèle thinks I should tell you. Naomi was crying on the phone. She wanted to know if I had seen you, or heard from you. She was worried, she said. She wanted to know how you were doing. I don't know, Tom. I'd say that she's a young lady that misses you quite a bit."

"Paul, do you really believe that Naomi could live like me?" Tom said.

"Well," Paul began, "I can't really say. I remember when you first moved up this way. You were building your cabin then, and living in a tent. You were trying to raise a team and all you had then were Oakie and Kimo. Remember how we talked about Oakie and how you doubted that she could ever lead a team. And Kimo, how all he ever wanted to do was fight. Look at your team now, Tom."

"Yes, Paul," Tom interrupted him, "but what does that have to do with anything?"

"Listen!" Adèle interjected sharply. "Listen to someone else for a change. You live alone too much. You see only one side. Go on, Paul. Tell him what you think."

"I don't know her that well," Paul said. He sat down on the arm of the stuffed chair next to his reading lamp. "I can tell you right now that any young lady who wants to live in the bush as much as she does, and especially with a guy who's afraid of losing his life in the bush as much as you are, well it seems to me that a match like that can't go wrong. Your wild team of Malamutes turned out right because you wanted them to be so. If you want something and you believe in it strongly enough, then things kind of take care of themselves. You just have to believe that."

"Yeah, I suppose," Tom said. He looked up at Paul, his best friend and mentor, a man whose advice he had never questioned. He turned towards Adèle; he saw only those brilliant brown eyes, that thin smile of confidence in her man, that he was right once again. This could be a tough trail ahead, Tom mused, a young woman wanting to live her life with him, with both Paul and Adèle on her side. He turned to his friend.

"I don't know, Paul," he said. "I just don't know."

Paul's eyes met those of Adèle's. To both of them, it was perfectly clear. They knew what this young man, Tom Franklin, was in for. They were as certain as if they themselves had organized the whole affair.

Paul breathed in deeply as he glanced from Adèle to Tom. Tom looked back at his friend in disbelief. He had the feeling that something was being finalized, that an agreement had just been reached and that there was nothing he could do to change it.

Paul smiled, a seemingly broad smile of accomplishment, and slapped his thighs with his large hands as he rose from the chair.

"Okay," said he said, "let's eat."

Acknowledgements

Many thanks to Robin Philpot (publisher) for his patience and constant encouragement. Without his help, this and the previous work, *Washika*, would never have come about. I also wish to express my gratitude to all of those people involved whom I have never met: graphic artists and designers, printers, all those responsible for the final product.